THE PEOPLE AND THE PROMISE

The People and the Promise

URSULA SYNGE

S. G. PHILLIPS New York

Copyright © Ursula Synge 1974
Map © The Bodley Head, Ltd. 1974
All rights reserved
Printed in the United States of America

Library of Congress Cataloging in Publication Data

Synge, Ursula, 1930-
  The people and the promise.

  SUMMARY: The Hebrew people's exodus from Egypt is
viewed through the eyes of Leah as she experiences it from her
childhood to old age.

  1. Jews—History—To 1200 B.C.—Juvenile fiction. 2. Mo-
ses—Juvenile fiction. [1. Jews—History—To 1200 B.C.—Fiction. 2.
Moses—Fiction] I. Title.
PZ7.S98465Pe   [Fic.]   74-10661
ISBN 0-87599-208-0

Introduction

The Egyptians, who recorded most things, left no record of the Exodus of the Hebrew people and nowadays even scholars disagree as to the Pharaoh in whose reign the event occurred, though Rameses II is the most generally accepted.

Without committing myself to one theory or another I have tried to reconstruct the Exodus in its historical time – somewhere in the late Bronze Age – to tell the story as it might have appeared to those who were living it, moving towards a new conception of a single, omnipotent god as surely as they were moving towards freedom and nationhood.

The Tribes of Israel, the children of El, had entered Egypt from Canaan many generations before, bringing with them their own religious beliefs and practices which were, in various but related forms, common to all the Semitic peoples. It was a world in which all matter was imbued with spirit, where every natural phenomenon was personified. Each important landmark – stone, well or tree – had its own El or spirit to whom the people of that locality looked for guidance and protection. There were also the gods of the hearth, personal gods attached to individual families; spirits of dead ancestors who were regarded as having a beneficial influence, their goodwill penetrating the barriers between the two worlds of life and death; and besides these there were demons who haunted the night and the waste places. There were the rites and ceremonies concerned with vegetation and the seasons, performed at sowing and harvest times. Of these the ritual drama of the death and resurrection of Tammuz or Dammuzi, the beloved of the goddess Ishtar, was widespread, enacted wherever crops were

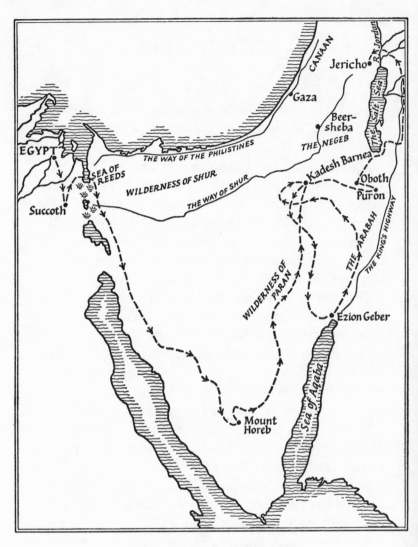

The journey to the land of the promise

raised. And there was the storm-god. In such regions as these, where drought might ruin one crop, and violent rains the next, the supreme god to be placated before all others was the god who governed the storm. He was like a wild bull, his bellowing was the thunder, his hooves struck lightning from the rocks A god of fertility, he impregnated the earth with his rains as the domestic ox impregnates the cows of the herd and fertilises the ground with his dung. He was a god of increase, but fierce, unpredictable and arbitrary.

The Kenites of the Sinai peninsula, who derived their name from Cain from whom they claimed descent, had worshipped such a storm-god, Yahweh, from a very early period. When Moses, returning from Sinai to Egypt, merged the cult of Yahweh with that of the El of Abram, a new stage in the development of the god began. He ceased to be a mere localised tribal god and began to evolve into the all-powerful and universal deity of later ages. This is not to say that the god changed, but that the understanding of his nature changed and developed as the people themselves changed. Moses, whether we regard him as magician, shaman, general, politician or priest, was the catalyst.

My concern has been with the people, how they were affected by the event in which they were caught up, what it meant to them and how it seemed to them at the time.

This, then, is a story with no individual hero or heroine, though I have used the eyes of an imagined woman, Leah, to guide me through the journey from the time when the Promised Land was no more than a hope for the future to the breaching of the walls of Jericho – so that I could really see the parched wilderness, and feel the heat and know what it was to be homeless and wandering for forty years.

I have been helped by many books, most particularly *Hebrew Religion* by W. O. E. Oesterley and Theodore H. Robinson,

7

and *Myth, Legend and Custom in the Old Testament* by Theodor Gaster. I should also mention Peake's *Bible Commentary*, *Egyptian Magic* by E. Wallis Budge, and *Hebrew Myths* by Robert Graves and Raphael Patai, and even then I would not have mentioned all. The tale of how Moses, when a military commander in Egypt, overcame the snakes is from Josephus' *History of the Jewish People*, and Baal-Shazzur's story of King Keret is from Canaanite mythology. Most reluctantly I omitted the marvellous tale of Balaam's ass because this could only have been added to the history at a later period; the immigrants could not have been aware of it at the time of its occurrence. And for similar reasons I did not begin with the well-known legend of Moses in the bullrushes; the miraculous preservation of the infant hero is the very stuff of folk-tale the world over and was, perhaps, included many, many years after the conquest.

THE PEOPLE AND THE PROMISE

I

For Leah the best times of all were those evenings when her father, having eaten and rested, would take her on his knee and hold her, safe and warm, against his broad chest while he talked. Sometimes she fell asleep and his voice ran on behind her dreams, comforting as wool, the words blurred together and lost, but at other times, when he talked especially to her, she would listen for as long as his voice lasted and not even blink her eyes.

The cooking fire glowed in the smoky dark and a small oil-lamp, raised on a shelf, burned before the squat clay figures that were the household gods. There was no other light inside the room but it was enough, for Rebekkah, Leah's mother, could spin in the dark, her quick, busy fingers drawing out the strands of combed wool, fitting them to the notch in her spindle, twisting, winding the thread on the shaft and drawing more wool, all in one movement with never a hesitation. Leah's lean grey cat, Bast, curled close to the mound of raw wool, asleep, one eye half-opened showing a line of gold, her whiskers twitching. Such was the pattern of the evening, permanent and unchanging – not like the pattern of the day that varied from one sunrise to the next.

Rebekkah was a small dark woman with an impatient tongue and hands that were quick to slap – and also quick to soothe. Leah loved her and feared her equally, but her father, Zorah, she loved without qualification. He was slow and gentle and always kind. Also he told wonderful stories about the past in which the Great Ones lived again, journeying across the distant hills with their flocks and herds, quarrelling, loving, marrying and raising children – from the day that Abram, the first ancestor, left his city of Ur until the time of Joseph when the Tribes came to rest here in Egypt. After that it seemed there were no more Great Ones, and no more history.

Zorah always ended that story with sadness in his voice which Leah, even when she was very small, thought strange, for surely it was a glad ending. All the brothers of Grandfather Joseph had come pouring into this land of Egypt to pitch their goatskin tents and even build houses on the land that Pharaoh had given them. She saw them as an everflowing stream of people spilling in from the desert waste with a great noise of singing and shouting, drums beating and horns blowing. What was there in that to make her father sad?

'Ah, that was in the old time,' he said, 'when the grass was green . . .'

Leah was a little older now and not afraid to ask questions when there was something she did not understand, though she still cast an anxious glance towards her mother. Rebekkah had a short way with interruptions.

'What happened?' Leah asked. 'You said the Pharaoh of those days loved our Grandfather Joseph – did he stop loving him? Did Pharaoh take away the grass?'

Could that be, she wondered. But only the gods could do that. All the green things withered and went under the ground when the god Tammuz died, and then the women, her own mother among them, went wailing into the fields, crying, 'Ah, Tammuz is dead! Our sweet brother!' It was a time of grief; nothing grew in the hard ground save stones, but later the god came to life again and the first green spears of barley pierced the earth, growing tall and golden in the sun's warmth. This was not what her father meant. 'What happened?' she asked again.

'You must not forget,' Zorah answered, 'that Grandfather

12

Joseph was one of twelve brothers. Think, Leah! Twelve tribes – with the wives and children and all their beasts, all the cattle, sheep and goats. How long before the grass was cropped to the soil? One generation? Two? Our first fathers moved from place to place, letting the pasture renew itself. Joseph's kinsmen and their descendants stayed. Perhaps, in our great pride, we thought that the El of Abram would renew the pasture for us, year after year. Who knows? But it was not renewed. Waiting, our people and their beasts grew thin together, for it seems that El's voice is not heard in Egypt.'

Then he told Leah how hunger came into the tents like a grey ghost to sit with the people, how famine stole the strength from the arms of the young men and withered the maidens in their first bloom.

'There is a hunger that comes with a poor harvest and passes away, but it was not like that. The rains fell in their due time, the sun shone, the Nile rose. The grass, where it grew, was sweet enough, but spare. This was a different hunger and it did not pass.'

Leah sat stiffly like a little carved Egyptian image, and listened.

'The people went to the old men, the wise men of the Tribes, and cried to them, "Speak to the god on our behalf. Tell him of our need!" But it was no use, Leah. The old men sat together, wagging their wise heads, but when they spoke it was of times past. And nothing was done. Then the young men met. They had no past to remember so they spoke, instead, of their patient wives and of the little ones whose bellies were swollen with emptiness, whose arms and legs were like sticks. These were the things they knew, and it was a knowledge they could neither endure nor escape. So they sold their land back to Egypt for little more than the right to live on it, and for a while there was no more hunger.'

He paused for a long time. Bast opened her yellow eyes wide, yawned and stretched, rolling onto her sleek back, claws extended to catch Rebekkah's flickering thread.

'And then?' Leah prompted.

'And then the hunger came back. The young men wept and the tears fell to their feet for now they had nothing to sell except their labour – so they sold that and their future with it – and the future of their children and their children's children.'

He put his big, gentle hands over her eyes and pressed her head close to him. 'Ah, Leah, may you never see a man weep so . . .'

My father has closed my eyes, Leah thought, that I may not see *him* weep. It is not the end of the story. She wriggled free and faced him squarely. It was true, the tears had dried on his cheeks but the fringes of his eyes were wet still and betrayed him.

'Are we slaves?' she asked, and found she could not bear to hear his answer after all. The room was so quiet, night and sorrow and loss filled all the space. The fire was too small to drive the shadows back; not even the magic of her mother's twisting thread could unsay the words, unthink the thoughts. But she had asked and Zorah would answer. She put her fingers in her ears so that she would not hear, but her father took both her hands and held them.

'We are *not* slaves,' he said, firmly. 'We have never been slaves. We are in bondage to Egypt – no more than that.' Remembering his tears, Leah wondered if bondage and slavery were so very different.

'It *is* different,' Zorah assured her. 'A slave is owned by his master – completely – body and spirit, as a beast is owned. His will is utterly given over, he is a possession – a thing. It is not so with us, though it is hard to remember the distinction as we work in the fields and brickyards, never enjoying the fruits of our toil. Yet, Leah, the distinction is there. When we are old and beyond work, we sit in the shade and think again of the heritage that is ours – the pact that Bull-El, El-Shaddai of the mountains, made with our first father Abram in the hills above the plain of Mamre . . .'

'Ah, that covenant!' cried Rebekkah, her face flushed and angry in the fire's light. 'It were better they forgot it entirely!' It was an old matter of contention between them, brought out and aired in every argument and even cherished for the spice it added to the knowledge each had of the other.

Now Zorah said, as he had said so many times before, 'Should we not remember the great times as well as the bad? Were we not honoured by the god's pact with Abram?'

'Honoured and afflicted – both! Believing in a promised land – a country where the rivers overflow with honey and the sky rains milk – we rear our sons and die in Egypt, in bondage, derided and despised. We talk of our heritage and the Egyptians laugh!' Rebekkah herself laughed but there was no mirth in it. The thread ran faster through her fingers. 'Though our father Joseph was twice and thrice beloved of Pharaoh, *we* are the least of the least . . .'

'Peace, Rebekkah! This Pharaoh who is styled Lord of the Two Lands and Son of the Sun, fears us.'

'So I have heard you say, husband.'

Rebekkah valued only what her eyes could see and her mind prove. The rough clay images that guarded her hearth showed their worth in a score of ways. They kept grain in the crock and water in the well, preserved the family and the beasts in health and protected them from the Evil Ones beyond the threshold. It would be foolish to neglect such gods as these – and worse than foolish to neglect the rites due to Tammuz, Lord of Vegetation, who died and rose again in the sight of all.

15

But Zorah, like all men, was a dreamer and it tried Rebekkah's patience sorely when he spoke with such pride of the ancient pact between Bull-El and Abram. Empty words! Let the god redeem his promise, let him lead the people away from Egypt and put the land of Canaan under their heel – then he would deserve their recognition and praise.

'Indeed great Pharaoh fears our people,' she said, ironically.

'It is the truth,' said Zorah. 'All men fear those they injure most, and their fear breeds hate and that hate, greater injury. It is as though our people and Pharaoh are bound together on a great wheel that turns without ceasing. Rebekkah, our two races were created in enmity even as the ibis is created the enemy of the serpent. The ibis devours the serpent that sucks her eggs – and the god, who made them both, has set them side by side so that each nurtures and destroys the other. Who questions this?'

'*I* question it! Egypt alone waxes fat while *our* people die!'

'All people die,' Zorah insisted. 'Even Egyptians die!'

'It is not the same. Who has ordered the killing of Egypt's first-born sons? I tell you, no man! Yet Pharaoh's soldiers have passed through *our* tents – aye – and more than once. Are you deaf, husband, that you have not heard? Are you blind? Did no one tell you how Pharaoh, the Son of the Sun, offered bribes to the Old Women that they should stifle *our* sons before even their first cries were heard?'

'I have heard that the Old Women of the Tribes were cunning as the serpent is cunning when the ibis walks abroad. I have heard that they took Pharaoh's bribes and told him that only daughters had been born in Goshen.'

'It is a woman's nature to rejoice in the birth of a son, to smile because the gods have smiled. Yet our women wept and sent their sons away to be reared in caves in the wilderness. Or hid them, fearfully, in store-houses, or in the straw that their

16

beasts trampled. Yet how many, do you think, were found and given to the crocodiles? How many?'

'Perhaps as many as were saved,' said Zorah, and he bowed his head low with grief for his neighbours' pains. 'But there are still enough of us left to people the promised land.'

So they argued – but Leah was asleep. Between the two wrangling voices she felt her consciousness drawn fine as her mother's thread until she dropped, spinning, into true sleep and heard nothing more.

The next day she took her cat with her and hid in the granary where she would not be able to hear her mother calling. Overnight her life had changed and, for the first time, Egypt was a strange country to her. She had loved the Nile as a true Egyptian loves it, rejoicing in its annual flood and the rich dark silt it left; in thankfulness she had thrown garlands to float on its surface and watched them drift slowly away. It had been her river and now it was so no longer. The Nile had no bounty for an Israelite child.

Richness and poverty were words she had always known, for the gods do not smile equally on all men. She had known that some were hungry and some were fed – this was in the nature of things. One man might own a single cow while another owned two and a third none at all. Yet there was no envy and no bitterness in such distinction. Sorrow and joy were the properties of all . . .

The cat, excited by the smell of mice and tormented by the grain-dust that prickled her nose, making her sneeze, hunted in the shadows, sometimes forgetting her prowling dignity to chase and catch her own tail. Yesterday Leah would have taken a straw and twitched it along the ground or through the air, encouraging the pretty beast to spring and pounce, laughing to see its pink, three-cornered gape and sharp white teeth – but between yesterday and today there stretched a world of difference.

She stood in the great doorway, a small scowling girl with tangled hair the colour of rust, and her thoughts went angrily to and fro between her old love for Egypt, the land that was hers and not hers, and her new-wakened love for the people whose gods had betrayed them into bondage.

Now the sun was low in the sky and the men of the Tribes were returning from their work in the clay-pits, walking slowly and dragging their feet along the rutted path as though the weight of the mud still clung to them. Leah ran to meet them and Zadkiel, her father's friend, a giant among men, lifted her and swung her up to ride on his shoulder. From such a height she thought it must be the whole of Egypt she could see, spread like a blanket fresh from the dyer's vat. It was not possible to imagine any land extending beyond the horizon, beyond the banks of the Nile, or beyond the desert. Her father often spoke of other cities to the South, cities that were larger and whiter and more dense with people, but he had never seen them and to Leah herself they were only tales told before sleep. Even the city she regarded as her own was an unfamiliar place, visited rarely, so far from the Hebrew settlement of tents and huts of mud and reeds each separated from its neighbour by a narrow plot of ground. Beyond the huts, between their teeming ways and the river, lay the barley field that provided grain for every household, to each man according to his family and need, and she had only to turn her head to see it all – the Place of the Dance, the field, the river, the wide road that led past the clay-pits to the city itself, the cultivated land and the wilderness that was peopled by demons and where the Egyptian dead slept in palaces of hewn stone, their faces masked with gold.

All this she saw as she had seen it a score of times before, but now, her eyes sharpened by misery, she saw much besides – the shoulders and backs of those who walked in front were criss-crossed over with fine, raised lines, scars and weals, many with the blood but lately dried – and she understood as surely as if the strokes had fallen upon her own body what the hippopotamus-hide whips the Egyptian overseers carried meant in terms of flesh, and what it was to be a Hebrew under Pharaoh's rule.

2

The days went by, and the moon changed and changed again. Bast grew slow and dignified, her face sharpened and her sides swelled. Then came a morning when she was nowhere to be found and Leah wept until Hannah, her closest friend who was two years older and very wise, said, 'Patience, stupid one!' and told her a marvellous, incredible tale. Sure enough, Bast came back after a while, thin and gaunt and carrying a squealing kitten in her mouth. Five journeys the cat made to her secret place, and five kittens tumbled underfoot until Rebekkah made Leah give them all away save one, a brindled male. When he was grown he went of his own accord and Leah was inconsolable.

'It is the way of the world,' said Zorah, comforting her. 'He has gone to find a wife of his own.'

'It is the way of the world,' he said again, some years later when his friend Zadkiel died of the coughing sickness, and he and Rebekkah went to mourn with the widow who sat in the furthest corner of her hut, hair unbraided and matted with dust.

Such grief was shocking to the young, a reminder that no person lives alone; every man's death kills something in another. Zadkiel had crossed the narrow threshold into the spirit-world and perhaps that was the end for him, but the step his wife took, from wifehood to widowhood, though it seemed as short, was but the beginning of another and bitter life.

'I shall never marry,' Hannah declared. 'I shall be like my cousin Miriam and serve the lady Ishtar with my whole life . . .'

'There is no law that says a priestess may not marry,' Leah answered. 'In fact they mostly do . . .'

'It is quite different. A priestess may change her husband as often as she wishes – and she mourns for none of them. Oh, Leah, I could not bear to break my heart for any man, or tear my cheeks with my own nails until the blood ran down. That is horrible!' She shuddered and put her hands to her face.

Leah said dreamily, 'I would not be afraid of loving for that reason. I will dance for the raising of Tammuz but I would not wear Ishtar's barley-crown – no, not if the god himself were to offer it.' She hugged herself and all the charms and amulets on her long brown arms clattered together. '*I* shall marry and have seven strong sons – but I shall take care to die before my husband. Then he will bargain for a field to be my burying-place as Grandfather Abram bargained with Ephron the Hittite for the cave of Machpelah that his wife Sarai should lie undisturbed . . .'

'You will need to make haste,' said Hannah, derisively. 'Men do not live so long in Egypt as Grandfather Abram did in the hills.'

So Hannah went to serve with Miriam, learning what must be done to bless the barley, and many other strange and secret things. And Leah stayed at home. She grew tall and straight, a modest, obedient girl, hard-working and soft-voiced, a daughter beyond price. Sighing, Zorah began to look about him for a suitable husband for his jewel. Many of his own kinsmen had sons of the right age and Rebekkah said, 'You have only to choose one from many; it does not matter which – they are all good men. Why do you make so much bother of it?' But Zorah shook his head and postponed a decision, thinking: Yes. This one is kind, his hands and his heart are open – but beggars flock to him like wasps to an orchard. How would my Leah

fare in her old age? Hadad will make his way in the world –
already he is as rich as an Egyptian – with him Leah would not
go hungry but he is, if anything, too shrewd. Now his brother
is handsome and children run to him for sweetmeats, he would
be merry even in adversity . . .

'It is not as simple a matter as you think, Rebekkah,' he said.
So he turned it about and about in his mind, deciding nothing
– until at last the gods, growing impatient, took a hand in it.

This came to pass at the Barley Feast when all the people of
Goshen put aside their working clothes and, bathed and newly-
clad, hurried to the Place of the Dance. This was a women's
feast, for the women planted the seed and gathered the harvest,
but all – men and women alike – shared in the joy of the
gathering as they shared the bread they ate.

The ground was cleared and swept, an altar set up at one end
with sheaves of barley laid upon it and flanked by two fires
from which other, lesser fires were kindled to light the dancers.
A little to one side the musicians sat and all the rest of the space,
save the area before the altar, was thronged with people, the
men a little aloof as though they had come only to please their
women, the women serious and apart.

The timbrel sounded, solemn as a heart-beat, the sistrum
whispered – then a sudden clash of the high-sounding cymbals,
and the sistrum's voice again but louder, joined by another.
Now came the Old Grandmother of the Tribes, the oldest and
wisest of all wise women. For three generations she had danced
the story of Tammuz, his death and resurrection, but age had
stiffened her joints and washed her eyes with the milk of blind-
ness so that she had to lean on Hannah's arm and go, halting,
to her place before the altar. This year it was Miriam who
reigned as Barley Queen.

The maidens, wearing the white of mourning and with their
long hair unbound, passed between the fires, their steps slow

and their bodies swaying, as the singer chanted: 'Tammuz is dead! Ah, mourn for Tammuz who has departed from us! Weep for Tammuz who dwells now in the house of Eresh-kigal, in the Land of No Return. Tammuz is dead, our sweet brother!'

As they danced Miriam walked among them, her head high and proud, her painted face as still as a stone. When she reached the centre of the floor, the dancers drew away and hid their faces. The music, save for the timbrel's insistent beat, was hushed. The singer chanted:

'The Lady abandoned heaven, abandoned earth,
    To the underworld she descended,
Abandoned lordship, abandoned ladyship,
    To the house of her sister, she descended,
    To Ereshkigal she descended.'

Then Hannah left the Old Grandmother's side and came forward to array Miriam like a queen, with a golden crown shaped like a wreath of barley, and a crimson robe fastened with two jewelled pins. A measuring rod was put into her hand, a necklace of blue stones about her neck, a gold ring on her finger and, last of all, a breastplate of gold. These were ancient treasures, brought to Egypt long ago, not by Joseph's people but by others who had once sought power in Egypt and found only bondage. Miriam bore their weight proudly though the wreath pressed on her temples and the breast-plate restricted her breathing.

Slowly she circled the floor, pausing seven times, at each stop removing one of the precious things and giving it back into Hannah's keeping while the music sighed and the singer, beating the rhythm on a hand-drum, intoned the story of Ishtar's descent and the words she spoke to Neti, the gatekeeper. Thus, one by one, Miriam gave up the trappings of royalty until she stood again, in only her white shift, before the altar. Here the Old Grandmother, robed in black as Ereshkigal, Ishtar's sister and Lady of the Underworld, waited to pronounce judgement on her.

> 'She fastened her eye upon her, the eye of death,
> Spoke the word against her, the word of anger,
> Uttered the cry against her . . .'

The cymbals clashed. Miriam stood, quite motionless, her head back, eyes closed. The dancers knelt with bowed heads, their hair sweeping the dust, for surely the whole earth must die now that Ishtar, as well as Tammuz, had gone from it. But the tale was not done. The grass withered and the trees dropped their leaves but Nin-shubar, Ishtar's vizier, lamented for her in the deserted groves and searched for her even in the house of the gods, in the dwelling-place of mighty Enlil – and Enlil's heart was touched by Nin-shubar's devotion. He sent his messenger to Ereshkigal, bearing rich gifts and promises so that the Lady of the Underworld had no choice but to let her sister go free again, and Tammuz after her, into the spring sunlight.

The maidens rose to their feet and danced again, wildly, tossing back their hair from bright faces, and Miriam, now crowned with a real barley wreath, led them.

It was at this moment that Ishvi, the third son of old Kedemah, the Wealthy One, came late to the dance, took one look at Leah's entranced face and could not look away. It is like that with some men; for them there is one only and no other. For Ishvi ben Kedemah, it was Leah. As soon as the dance was finished he crossed the floor to seek out her father.

Zorah went home that night well pleased, not only with himself but with all the world. Already in his mind he counted his grandchildren and they were as numerous and as shining as the stars in the sky – shepherds and herdsmen and kings – descendants of Abram, inheritors of the promise . . .

But later, when he told Rebekkah what had passed between himself and the son of Kedemah, she merely clicked her tongue and said, 'That is not the way such things are arranged, my husband. This young man should have spoken first to his father; then Kedemah would have come to you in due time. Between you two should it have been decided and gifts exchanged. That is the proper way that time and custom have honoured. Well, what did you say to him?'

Zorah felt the pride go out of him. Rebekkah was right. Shame-faced, he replied, 'I told him I would speak to my daughter and learn her mind.'

Rebekkah whirled round, her voice sharp with indignation. 'Indeed? That is something new. And what experience of life has our daughter that she should be capable of choosing a husband for herself?'

'Peace, Rebekkah! I have not asked that she choose a man for herself; only that she may say "No," to one that displeases her. Is that so terrible a thing?'

His wife relented a little and dimples showed in her faded cheeks. 'For Leah, who is a sensible girl, perhaps not. But it would be a dangerous custom to follow. Think how many plain, honest men would be passed over because a maiden's dreams were of one with the face and form of Tammuz! Supposing I had said "No" to you, Zorah?'

That was an answer gentle enough to gladden any man's heart, but Zorah had more to say and once it was said he feared it would be a long time before he saw his wife smile again. And even as he hesitated the smile fled away.

'But why do we discuss it at all?' she cried. 'Is Ishvi the first son of old Kedemah? Or even the second? No, my husband, he is the third son, the child of his old age. What has he to commend him as a son-in-law beyond a good heart and a willingness to work?'

'Neither of these things is a small consideration, wife.'

'I grant you! But – for Leah? No! I will say no more. Let there be an end to it.'

Rebekkah wrapped herself in the blanket and turned her back on him. Zorah scratched meditatively in his beard. The worst was still to come. Timidly he touched his wife's shoulder. 'I have spoken with Leah,' he said. There was no response. He said again, a little louder, 'I have spoken with Leah.'

Rebekkah raised herself on one elbow. 'I thought I had not heard you right. I thought I dreamed. I did not know I had married such a fool. *You* have spoken to Leah already? Would the morning not have done as well? But no! Straight from the feasting you must speak to her . . .'

'It was the barley wine,' he admitted sorrowfully, and Rebekkah made an angry noise in her throat that was like spitting.

'We were all so happy,' he said. 'The words slipped out before I knew they were in my mouth to say.'

'Then the damage is done,' said Rebekkah, and her voice was quiet, her hands still. 'What said our daughter?'

Zorah's heart swelled with pride. What should a daughter answer to such a question as he had put to her? A good daughter, trained in modesty and obedience by a good mother? 'She said, "If such a match pleases my father, then it also pleases me." '

'Good,' said Rebekkah, once again preparing herself for sleep. 'Then no more need be said.'

'Rebekkah, I told her that it pleased me well.'

For two days the woman went about with her mouth set in an obstinate line – and then gave in. Ishvi was a good young man, serious and well-mannered; he would make a fine husband, as Zorah had done. After all, Zorah had not been rich either. Steadiness – that was the quality to respect in a husband. A rich man had everything to lose, a poor man everything to gain. Having accepted what could not be changed, she blamed Zorah for delay in the affair. 'My husband,' she scolded, 'have you not invited Kedemah to eat with us? Surely you have a matter to discuss with him.'

So Kedemah came to meat and Rebekkah greeted him kindly, even chiding him a little for not visiting them before. Leah brought water for the guest's hands, blushing as he looked keenly at her from under his white brows, which pleased him, for modesty, he thought, was a virtue not often found in these later days. All day the girl had worked beside her mother, stewing a young kid with wild garlic, and shaping and baking bread; now she retired into the shadows while Rebekkah sang her praises: 'This bread my Leah made. In the whole of Israel there is no maiden of her age who has such a light touch with bread. And it is always the same, never too pale, never burnt. Eat, Kedemah, and know for yourself what a prize your son will gain.'

Kedemah ate, dipping his fingers into the great dish while Rebekkah pointed out for him the most succulent pieces. 'It is well enough,' he said cautiously. Too good for Ishvi, he thought – but that was something they all knew. Well, he would not shame his son.

'Ishvi is not my first-born,' he added, 'yet I value him. When he marries I shall miss his strong arms.' He paused. 'Moreover I am not rich . . .'

Zorah hid the smile that sprang too quickly to his lips. He shrugged and spread his hands wide. 'Who of our people is rich?' he asked. 'If you know such a one, name him. Our service is to Pharaoh, mine as well as yours, Ishvi's with his

27

brothers'. Therefore let us not speak of riches but of our young people. In our grandchildren, Kedemah, lies the hope of our race.'

'Even so. Yet our fathers kept their herds and, in our bondage, it is good to remember that. We will not bargain as slaves, Zorah, but as free men.'

Zorah looked to his household gods for assurance. In the dim, wavering light they seemed to nod encouragement.

'With Leah I will give a white cow,' he said. 'I have such a one among my few poor beasts, and it shall be hers on her wedding-day.'

'With Ishvi I will give a goat,' said old Kedemah, the Wealthy One. 'Two goats,' he corrected himself, not to be outdone in generosity, though he winced as he said it. 'A male and a female.'

Zorah turned to his wife and again spread his hands, wide enough now to embrace the whole of Israel, its past and whatever future the gods had planned for it. 'The beginning of a herd,' he cried. 'Surely these children of ours are blessed!' He closed his eyes to hold back the tears of joy that threatened to overflow and saw, behind his lids, the vision of a fair green valley where fat cows wandered at will while the surrounding hills echoed with the bleating of Ishvi's goats as they browsed among the tamarisks, tended by Leah's healthy sons. What did it matter that reality at this moment meant only two scrawny goats and one young cow? The rest would come as surely as the great Nile flooded its plains each year.

'They will have milk and cheese,' said Kedemah, dryly. 'And that is something in these harsh days.'

The feast in honour of the barley drew to its close. On the last night Leah, crowned with a circlet of the golden grass, joined hands with Ishvi, crossing the division between her family and his, becoming a daughter of his father's house. Rebekkah held her close, weeping as though it were for the last time.

'Many sons, beloved child. Many strong sons,' she said. 'An old woman lives again in her grandchildren.' Leah, herself near tears, had already forgotten her mother's stinging slaps and continual rebukes, remembering only the comforting voice that had soothed away pain and night-fears alike. But now she too was grown, a married woman, and it was not seemly to cling to the past. Gently she freed herself and moved away but Rebekkah followed her, taking from her own neck the fine gold chain hung with amulets and putting it about Leah's neck, saying, 'This my mother gave me on the day I wed Zorah, your father, and she had it from her mother. Take it, may it preserve you both in joy, one with another, as it has done with us.'

Then the crowd parted them for it was time to carry the Harvest Lord, the last sheaf from the reaping, in procession to the field, to be torn asunder and scattered that next year's harvest might be as rich. The torches flared and smoked, making a canopy of red-hued cloud above the heads of the celebrants as they wound their way, chanting, between the huts. Their voices carried far in the still air.

3

That day in the city had also been one of feasting, but with a different cause. The lordly Egyptians, being more concerned with conquest than with the barley god, celebrated the recent victory of Prince Ra-Mose over the Ethiopians.

'A grave occasion,' Prince Ra-Mose said. 'I would rather fight a score of such campaigns than endure another civic welcome.'

He had been greatly honoured by his kinsman, Pharaoh; gifts filled his treasure-house and his new titles still resounded in his ears like a roll call of all the gods – yet it wearied him. Therefore he had excused himself from Pharaoh's table and dined instead in private luxury with his friends, Ka-Maat and Sekhenmut. Now they reclined at their ease on the terrace of Sekhenmut's house, a slave making music on the double-pipe, and the wine passing from hand to hand.

Prince Ra-Mose sighed contentedly. 'I will buy your cook from you, Sekhenmut. You have only to name your price.'

'Many have offered,' answered Sekhenmut, 'but even to you I must say, "The man is not for sale." I also like to eat. And besides – of what use is a cook like mine to a soldier?'

'A soldier?' Ka-Maat questioned. 'Or a god? In this last victory Ra-Mose has stepped beyond the bounds of ordinary men. You might have feasted him as well on the smoke of incense and sweet-smelling wood . . .'

'Yet he eats like a man. Come, Ra-Mose, tell us what a man must do to be praised so in his own life-time.'

Ra-Mose carefully selected a ripe fig from the platter at his elbow, peeled it slowly and bit into the purple flesh.

'It is scarcely worth the telling – a stratagem so simple that any man might have thought of it ... except a soldier,' he added.

'How so?'

'A soldier is bred to discomfort. He is so used to wounds and stench and meat that crawls with worms that he notices them no more than he notices the fatigue of his body or the heat of the noon sun. Each trade has its disadvantages, my friends, and a man who wishes to do well must adjust himself to them. But *I* saw what a more experienced soldier does not see – that discomfort is wasteful of good men. We were losing lives as carelessly as a man spills sand between his fingers. Yet where there is water a wound may be cleansed, not left to fester until the limb drops off or the man dies. I also learned that if we made our place of easement beyond the camp we were less troubled by flies and lost fewer men to the running sickness in the belly ...'

'It was for digging ordure-pits that Pharaoh honoured you?'

Ra-Mose chose another fig. 'Ah, no! That was chiefly for my victory over the serpents, I think.'

'The serpents?' Ka-Maat rose and removed the dish. 'You shall eat no more until you deal honestly with your friends. What does Pharaoh care for serpents?'

'He cares for victory. The whole land to the south of Egypt is alive with snakes. Their venom is deadly – no water on earth can rinse it away. Having such guardians, the tribes beyond the frontier need no walls to keep them safe from Pharaoh's anger ...'

He reached again for the figs but Ka-Maat retreated with the dish. 'Are there no amulets against snake-bite?'

'A man might be so hung about with charms he could not set one foot before the other by reason of their weight, yet be bitten, turn black and die where he stood.' Ra-Mose made a

31

hideous grimace, his lips drawn back and his tongue protruding between his teeth. 'The figs, I implore you,' he groaned. Ka-Maat yielded.

'But your story halts as often as a funeral procession,' he warned. 'Already our host is yawning. How did the Lord Ra-Mose, Beloved of the Gods, placate the Lady of Serpents?'

'I called the men back and we retreated to the river ...' Pausing, he heard again the grumbling of the men, schooled to march only forward though they died in their ranks, and the taunts of the warrior lords who were his peers. 'I thank all the gods that the command was mine,' he said. 'Had it been otherwise my skull would now be decorating some Ethiop's tent-pole, grinning at the buzzards. And most especially do I thank Ibis-headed Thoth who gave me some small share of wisdom ...'

'So Pharaoh honoured you because you retreated to the river, thus avoiding the serpents. This is not the story they tell in the market-place. There I heard of a captured city and a tribute of spears and slaves.'

Sekhenmut roused himself. 'I will finish it for him,' he said. 'He will draw out the tale till dawn if we let him. He set his men to weaving reed baskets with lids – and in the baskets they carried ibises, the birds of Thoth. When they reached the region of the serpents, they released the birds – the snakes fled. The ibises hunted and feasted well. The army marched free. You see, it is quickly told.' He clapped his hands and called for more wine, but Ka-Maat stayed him. 'This wine of the north is good,' he said, 'but have you no wine of the Oasis? Surely such a victory deserves the best.'

A slave came, soft-stepping as a cat, and refilled each goblet. The talk drifted and died. Now the distant chanting of the Israelites could be heard quite plainly. Prince Ra-Mose raised his head and listened; a small breeze stirred the hair at the back of his neck and he shivered. He crossed the terrace and stood looking over the tilled land to where the lights of the procession moved at the edge of the marshes.

'What are those people?' he asked. 'Surely they do not celebrate Pharaoh's victories in Goshen?'

Ka-Maat stood at his shoulder. 'They are the Hebrew,' he said, indifferently. 'They celebrate the harvest. For seven idle days they have feasted, with songs and dancing; tonight they scatter the broken barley-god about their field. Tomorrow they work again. They are a people in bondage to Egypt.'

Ra-Mose shivered again, more violently, and his hand that held the goblet shook so that wine spilled on the fine white linen of his garment. 'The Hebrew,' he said. 'Yes, I have heard of them. They regard themselves as a chosen race, sealed and set aside from other men by a covenant between some distant ancestor of theirs and a mountain-god of Canaan.' He laughed. 'So it is said – yet they are far from the land that gave them birth and it would seem that this god has forgotten them.'

'And they, him,' said Ka-Maat. 'Or why do they praise the barley?'

'Come, let us find out.' These words, spoken impulsively, he regretted at once for it was agreeable to sit here in the cool night air, bathed, fed and at peace; in the Hebrew quarter there would be noise and the stink and press of people – but the words were said, it would be a sign of weakness to recall them. Sekhenmut sprawled half-asleep on his gilded couch. He would not accompany them, he said. Distance lent magic to the rites, proximity would soon stale. Ka-Maat privately agreed but already Ra-Mose was calling for a torch to lead them.

The Israelites were dispersing to their homes, lingering over last farewells, when they saw the two Egyptian lords approach. Old Kedemah spat to his right and left to avert whatever evil their presence might bring. 'These Egyptians!' he muttered.

'Princes of night and sorcery, what trouble do they now bring upon us that not even our feast is sacred?'

Hamor, his second son, spoke softly, venomously. 'They are a blight on our feasting, like the brown stain that spreads through the ripe barley when the gods are angry. Let us do with them as we would with the spoiled crop. Let us kill!'

A murmur of assent ran through the crowd, but no man stirred; each waited for his neighbour to move first and, though their ears were Hamor's, they looked to Aaron for guidance and would not move without his consent. This Aaron was a headman among them, a wise man who sat in council with the elders of the Tribes. It was said that El spoke with him and had taught him the art of healing, and many other things beyond the knowledge of ordinary men. Because of this he was honoured as a priest is honoured. Now he stood firm and still, and it was as though Hamor had never spoken, as though the murmur had never been. There would be no killing that night.

Ka-Maat felt their hatred like a blow delivered at his back; he felt it physically the way a beast does when it balks at a shadow. Ra-Mose felt it too, but pleasurably. It was a challenge he recognised – the hatred a conquered people bears towards its master. The men drew back from him, silent now and oppressed in their spirits, and Ra-Mose walked along the path they cleared for him, his nose wrinkling at the combined smells of their woollen garments and barley ale and the sputtering oil of the torches.

Aaron stepped forward to greet him. 'Life! Health! Strength!' he said, bowing to the ground and speaking in the Egyptian tongue. His words offered conventional respect to Pharaoh and to all Egypt, but his voice was ironic and amused. Doubt flickered in the Prince's mind. Fear and hatred he knew

34

how to meet, but this was altogether new in his experience – that a man whose condition was little better than a slave's should greet him almost as an equal. It was as though the Hebrew invited him to scoff at Egypt's might and power, as though he said, 'Let us give Pharaoh his due for he is a child who needs the security that ritual bestows. But come, we are men, you and I. We know better.'

Ra-Mose frowned, putting his hand to the gold and lapis scarab he wore pendant on his breast, reminding himself that in this place *he* was Egypt. Ka-Maat touched his shoulder. 'We shall learn nothing here, Prince,' he said. 'Let us go back to our wine.'

Without looking at him, Ra-Mose answered, 'Go back. I shall stay a while.' When Ka-Maat hesitated, not liking to return alone lest harm come to the Prince and he be blamed for it, Ra-Mose said again, 'Go back.' It was an order.

Ka-Maat put his hand to his forehead and lips in token of his submission and went. Ra-Mose turned to Aaron and said, 'Send these people away.' When they were alone together he smiled and said, 'I think you must be the priest. You have not the bearing of a slave.'

Aaron answered, 'I am Aaron, the son of Amram, the son of Levi. Why should I bear myself like a slave?'

Ra-Mose bowed. 'I am Ra-Mose, the son of Osiris,' he said and the Hebrew, looking into the Prince's arrogant young face, could well believe that indeed no being less than a god had fathered him.

'Osiris has a distinguished son. His fame is known even here, even among my people who have no cause to rejoice when Pharaoh adds another province to his dominion. But what brings my lord, the son of the god Osiris, to Israel's tents?'

Ra-Mose shrugged. 'I saw your lights. I heard your chanting. Curiosity led me here and that alone. Or if there be a deeper reason perhaps you know of it. Chance, they say, is a servant of the gods.'

Aaron led the Prince to his house, a humble place of clay and reeds, in no way different from a score of others. A woman, who had been sitting near the fire, nursing a child, rose when they entered and went into the inner room, returning almost at once with a skin of wine and some barley cakes which she offered the guest without speaking.

Ra-Mose drank and repressed a shudder, for the wine was thin and sour, fit only to quench thirst in the heat of the day. But the cakes were good and the water in which he cleansed his fingers was cool as though new-drawn from the well.

'Now tell me,' he said, as Aaron in his turn set the wineskin down, 'about your people and why they, being – as I have heard – the chosen of one god, celebrate the resurrection and the reaping of another?'

The fire was very low, no more than a red glow in the dark, the shadows creeping in from the walls to extinguish it. In the inner room a child cried out and was hushed.

Aaron said, 'Do not all people praise the barley? It is a mystery our women carried with them from the east, a dance of death and regeneration, these matters being closest to a woman's being. Who can mourn Tammuz as is most fitting? Who but a woman can wear Ishtar's crown and majesty that the earth may flourish again?'

'But that other god – the god of your covenant?'

'Ah, that is an old history. Many generations have been born and lived and been laid to their rest since the Great Spirit sealed his pact with our father Abram. Our people await the deliverer who will lead them into the land of the promise – and, meanwhile, we praise the barley as is the way of hungry men, whatever their gods. But, Prince of Egypt, we have not forgotten the Great Spirit, Bull-El, the begetter of life. We remember him, as of old, in the patient ox that draws the plough, and rejoice whenever a bull-calf is born. Does that answer you?'

Ra-Mose considered the other's words and it seemed to him that this was but a savage god, such as the outland people worship. Had they no great one to set beside Amon-Ra, god of the life-giving sun? For let the plodding ox drop his dung in the furrows, let the rain fall as it will – the barley does not ripen unless the sun warms the seed.

'These are gods of the belly,' he said, flatly. 'No more than that! What of Thoth, lord of all wisdom, he who first measured time? What of ram-headed Khnemu, the fashioner of gods and men? What of Osiris who rules beyond the grave?'

Aaron shook his head. ' Prince Ra-Mose,' he said, 'was not your Osiris, long ago, a lord of vegetation, his limbs divided and scattered? Did not Isis, the Lady, seek and gather them one by one, even as Ishtar sought her beloved and won him from Ereshkigal, the Queen of the Underworld? But perhaps you Egyptians in your palaces of brick and stone have forgotten that? What do you remember of your origins? The tall columns of your halls are like lotus-stems and the capitals that crown them are like the flowers of the lotus – but they are stone, Prince Ra-Mose. Whatever your feet tread now, it is not earth. Osiris may rule as king in the realms of the dead, but he was once something other . . .'

So they talked and the fire died, unheeded. When at last the Prince rose to leave, Aaron accompanied him to the doorway and stood with him under the stars.

'I came to learn something of your gods,' said Ra-Mose, 'yet it seems you have told me of my own. Now tell me, is such wisdom as yours also the gift of the Bull? Or is there another and greater god of whom you do not speak?'

'What man reveals his treasure all at once? And to a stranger? You are an Egyptian, a nobleman, beloved of Pharaoh. Idleness turned your footsteps hither, an impulse born of wakefulness and the warm night. What did you hope to find, Prince? A common wizard such as every tribe possesses, a maker of amulets and interpreter of dreams? I am not such a one, and any wisdom that I have is indeed the gift of Bull-El. If you would learn more of my people and their gods, you will come again . . .'

So they parted, but Aaron stood in thought for a long while after the Prince had left him. He felt there had been something momentous in their encounter – the stars and the season together were auspicious of good, great good – yet he was uneasy. That stain on the Prince's robe – surely it was like blood and signified danger, but whether to the Prince or to Israel, he could not tell.

His wife, Elishabeta, came out to him with the child still in her arms. 'He will not sleep,' she said, reproachfully. 'The noise of the feast disturbed him and he is in pain with his great teeth. I have rubbed his gums with the bitter herb and poured out grain to the gods of the hearth, but nothing quiets him. I have waited long for you.'

Aaron took the child from her and held him against his shoulder, brushing back the damp tendrils of hair from the hot forehead. With one finger he stroked his son's reddened cheek, and the pain wriggled like a worm into his own flesh. He drew his hand away and shook it. The child breathed easily and slept.

'Why did the Egyptian come?' Elishabeta whispered. 'Why did you admit him to our house? We shall be accursed because of it, the children will sicken and the beasts die. What did he want of you?'

'I am not sure. What any man needs of another, perhaps, to

know that he is not alone. The true reason is not yet revealed, but he will come again. Of that I am sure.'

'He stifles my breath,' said Elishabeta. 'Do not welcome him, I beg you.'

'It is not in my power to turn him away,' Aaron said, 'either now or at any time. Egypt may yet have a gift for Israel and who knows but that this man may bring it?'

4

During the following days Prince Ra-Mose stayed away from the Hebrew quarter altogether. His words with Aaron faded as a dream fades after waking. These people were no concern of his, he thought. Then, returning from a day's hunting, he met with a party of Hebrew workmen dragging a granite block from the quarry. They were roped together like beasts, and like beasts, strained at the ropes, their muscles responding to the crack of a whip. Ra-Mose averted his eyes from them as he rode by for he felt shame such as he had not known before. The hawk on his wrist, though chained and hooded, flying only at his command, had more dignity than these toiling men, or than those who drove them. He was ashamed to be a man . . .

And that night he visited Aaron again and, squatting down on the earth floor, said: 'Now tell me about your god and why he has abandoned his people.'

'Tonight I will make a beginning,' Aaron said.

Night after night the Prince sat by Aaron's fire, and learned the history of the Hebrew race from the creation of the earth when El conjured the land from chaos and moistened it with his breath to make it fruitful. He learned of Adam, the first father of all men, and of Eve, his woman, who worshipped a serpent and brought sin into the new, green world. And he learned of Noah, in whose lifetime El sent a flood to destroy all living things because of the evil that was in them, and saved only Noah with his wives and sons, bearing them safely above the waves in a wooden ark. And he learned at last of Abram who had walked with El on the hilltops and made a covenant with him, ratified by the blood of sacrifice.

'And this was your same god? This was Bull-El?'

'How shall a man conceive of a god,' asked Aaron, 'save in what he knows? Do we not see about us every day the works of the bull, his strength and majesty? Does not the earth bring forth in greater abundance where the bull has trod?'

'Yet I think he has abandoned you,' Ra-Mose answered.

'We are only men and live for a few short years and die. That is nothing in the life of a god. Our children or our children's children will inherit, Prince.'

Ra-Mose answered nothing to this, for such an attitude was beyond his understanding, that people should accept their hardship with meekness and make no effort to overcome the evil that encompassed them. Wryly, he saw himself as a part of that evil and wondered how it was he went so safely among the Hebrew, why no one crept behind him in the dark . . .

'They hate me,' he said, 'and with cause since I am an Egyptian. Why do they not kill me and thus have done with at least one of their oppressors?'

'It is not our way. El is mightier than all men; he will smite the Egyptians when the time is right.'

Ra-Mose smiled. 'Yet, if I were of your race, I would kill.' And his smile took the edge from his words, making a jest of them.

One evening, as they talked together, a man came and spoke quietly to Aaron who rose to his feet at once, saying, 'Go on before me. I will be with you shortly.' Then, turning to Ra-Mose, he said, 'I must leave you, Prince. A man is dying – one I have known and honoured all my life. Do not wait for me.'

'I will come with you.'

'You can do no good there.'

'Nevertheless, I will come.'

'It is not wise. A year ago this man's son died, leaving a widow and four young children to fend for themselves. Laban was old, he had earned his rest, but he took his son's place in the clay-pits that his grandchildren should not starve. Now he too is dying. You will not be welcome in that house, I tell you.'

'Unless you forbid me, I will come. Am I to know only one side of Israel?'

Already people were gathering at the door of Laban's house and they looked resentfully at Ra-Mose as he followed Aaron inside but no voice was raised against him; such was the protection Aaron's company gave.

The old man lay on a couch in the inner room. The sweat of death was upon him and, though his daughter-in-law constantly wiped his face and breast, it sprang again from his pores in the same moment so that her task was useless save for the love there was in the performance of it. Aaron raised him in his arms and blessed him, calling upon El to deal tenderly with him in the After-world. Ra-Mose saw the bruises and welts on the emaciated body and anger and pity gripped him like twin demons. He could not stay listening to the labouring breath, but turned and left the house.

'Was there no one else to care?' he demanded. And a young man answered, 'There is always someone to care, but each cares first for his own. Laban was a strong man once and, in his age, unwilling to give the responsibility for his son's family into another's keeping . . .'

'A strong man!' said Ra-Mose. 'A sack of bones!'

'A fine man,' insisted the other, 'and not so long ago. But his eyes failed him and he grew slower. Indeed, what man quickens with age? Yesterday he fell and could not rise at once. The overseer was enraged – ' He shrugged. 'When he had done whipping him and it was useless, he kicked him – and that was useless too. It broke his ribs, I think.'

Ra-Mose bit his lips until the blood came. 'Who did this thing?'

'It was Seteki, the overseer,' and others nodded and said, 'Aye, Seteki, Pharaoh's beast.' Then one said, 'What is it to you, Prince? One labourer the less! But his place will be filled, never worry!' and he stooped to pick up a stone.

The Prince felt a hand on his arm and a voice said, close to his ear, 'Do not stay, Prince. Grief has made them savage but it is not for you to pay for this old man's death. Go back to the city, and they will forget – but go now.'

'I will send food for the woman and her children. What more can I do?'

'It is enough.'

'Tell Aaron. Say that I have gone to attend to it.'

'I will tell him.'

'But wait – what is your name?'

'Are you afraid I will not carry your message? I am Ishvi ben Kedemah. Be assured that I will tell Aaron where you have gone and on what business. But go now, Prince. If they stone you, it will be the worse for them.'

And Ra-Mose said again, as he had said to Aaron, 'If I were a man of your race, I would kill!' but this time there was no jesting in his smile.

5

Leah and Ishvi were happy during these next years. The gods of the hearth-place smiled on them. The white cow that was Leah's bride-portion bore a bull calf and that was a portent of greater good to come, for Leah herself was soon big with child. The old women gathered round her, bringing gifts and advice, while Rebekkah darted hither and thither among them, scolding and harrying, jealous that any advice but hers should ease her daughter's travail. 'Peace, Rebekkah!' they protested. 'A child is for Israel.' But Rebekkah would hear nothing of that. 'A child is for the grandmother!' she declared, and to Leah she said, 'Give me a grandson, my daughter, that I may hold a man-child in my arms.' Leah forced a smile to her mouth, gasping as the pain took her. Later, when she showed her son to Ishvi, she said, 'When my hour was upon me I was not brave enough to disobey my mother.'

Everything in their household prospered. The first child was a boy, the second a girl and they were both plump, even-tempered babies, readier to laugh than to cry, even when they tumbled against stones or a dog snapped at them in the heat. Rebekkah herself could find no fault with such children nor in the way her daughter was rearing them. Deprived of that grandmotherly duty she set herself to boast among the other matriarchs until they threw up their hands and vowed such paragons could not exist, and went grumbling back to their own daughters who bore ordinary babies who wept and fretted.

Men spoke of Ishvi with respect as a man who made things grow. His bull calf was sold for a good price, his she-goat bore twin kids, both female. Even Kedemah, who admitted little good in the world, began to think that Zorah had not been so far wrong when he spoke of the future on the night of Leah's betrothal.

Of his other sons Kedemah was less sure. Micael, the eldest, was a good man, upright in his dealings – but not lucky. If a crop failed, it was Micael's; if a cow took milk-fever and died, it was Micael's cow. If a house sagged and collapsed for whatever reason, it was Micael's family that found itself homeless. Without any intention on his part he was a constant drag on his father's purse-strings. Yet he was a better son than Hamor.

Hamor was a rebel. As a youth he had rebelled against his father; as a man he rebelled against the officers and overseers of Pharaoh. He was restless and dangerous; where he went trouble followed for he had a golden tongue that stirred the blood of others – yet the gods protected him. He collected about him many kindred spirits, young men who called themselves 'Sons of the Bull', who secretly practised with weapons, waiting for the day of blood-letting to arrive. The people trembled when he passed, for surely he would bring down the wrath of Pharaoh upon them all, innocent and guilty alike. But when the Egyptians came searching among the tents and houses for Hamor, no one knew his whereabouts. He was here and there and not there, like a wind, like smoke. No one betrayed him.

'Ah, you should get him a wife,' said Rebekkah, 'find him a good girl like my Leah. Then he would settle and we would all sleep sound again. That is what a young man needs. Without a wife he is like meat without salt, like bread without leaven . . . Let him have sons of his own to fear for and you will see how quiet he becomes, how eager to pass unnoticed.'

'But who,' demanded Kedemah, 'would give a daughter to

Hamor? Would you? Not if you had ten daughters!'

It could not be denied. Neither Rebekkah nor any other mother among the Tribes would have welcomed Hamor into her family, but that did not grieve him. He did not feel in himself the need for a wife; suspicion fed him and hatred kept him warm. Impartially he hated Egypt, her whole people and all her gods – but in particular he hated one man, and one he suspected before all others. The man he hated was Seteki, the overseer in the brickfields, a beast whose very grunt spoke death; the man he distrusted was Prince Ra-Mose.

'He is a spy,' he reasoned. 'Why otherwise should he go to and fro between his race and ours? What friendship,' he spat the word, 'can a master have with a slave?'

'He visits Aaron,' said Leah, wearily for she had heard this argument many times before. 'Aaron is no slave . . .' and Ishvi added, 'There are no slaves among our people, brother. Bondsmen, it is true, and labourers, but no man is a slave unless he feel it here and here.' He touched his brow and breast. 'Five days of every seven I owe to Pharaoh, the work of my hands and the strength of my back, to build a palace for him to lie in when the embalmers have done. But I am not Pharaoh's thing, Hamor.'

Leah turned to her husband with anxious eyes. 'Yet there *is* the smell of danger about him, Ishvi. We should not trust too much . . .'

Hamor paused in his restless pacing and caught his brother by the sleeve. 'Heed your woman,' he said. 'I tell you that many of our people will die because of this man.'

But Leah was not to be drawn into too close an alliance with such a firebrand as Hamor. A little way was far enough. 'And many of our people may die because of *you*,' she said, tartly. 'If, as you think, Prince Ra-Mose is a spy, you would do well to avoid him. If trouble comes, it will be through you and your friends. Remember, when you play at warriors, that we are no great multitude to resist an army.'

'We are enough,' said Hamor, 'if we be but roused.'

'I will speak with Aaron,' sighed Ishvi, when Hamor had left them. 'Perhaps my brother is right. Perhaps we should all guard our tongues when the Prince is among us. Who knows what matters a man might reveal, unknowing, or what an alien mind can make of a small phrase, imperfectly understood?'

Aaron heard him with a grave face. Such words had a familiar ring. Hamor had spoken them angrily and more than once; Micael also had warned him; Zorah and Kedemah had come together and spoken no less urgently, and so had a score of other men. To all of them he had answered the same thing: 'This Egyptian is not like the rest. You need have no fear of him.' And when they persisted, he said, 'Enough, he is my brother!'

And Ra-Mose continued to frequent the by-ways of Goshen, now calling at other dwellings besides Aaron's, and speaking of other matters than the gods. Laban's daughter-in-law was not the only one he helped, but his gifts were accepted reluctantly, and his presence no more than tolerated. The women, particularly, feared him and, when he had gone away, rated their husbands for being too open with him. Only the children liked him, as children will welcome anything that is strange – and with them he relaxed a little, displaying a side of his nature that their parents never saw.

But it was not only in the Hebrew quarter that the Prince's friendship with the priest was viewed askance, it was also a matter of grave concern to his closest companions in the city. At first it had amused them to mock him, calling him Ra-Mose the Hebrew, or declaring that he had become enslaved by a slave, that in Goshen some gazelle-eyed beauty beckoned. But as time passed and still the Prince's infatuation stayed, they grew anxious for him and conspired together to keep him occupied in ways more fitting to his station. Abandoning their own indolent habits they arranged hunting expeditions in the desert, or floundered about with him in the marsh hurling boomerangs to bring down the wild birds that nested there. And Ra-Mose hunted with them, and speared fish and raced his chariot against theirs – but the next day, or the day after, he was to be found in Goshen once again, sitting at Aaron's feet in the airless room, never minding the oppressive heat.

At last Ka-Maat brought his fears into the open. 'I suspect that you are watched,' he said. 'Perhaps not always, but more often than you think. Such friendships as you profess are not to be encouraged, Ra-Mose.'

The Prince scowled. His face, reflected in the still fish-pool, scowled back at him, a dark and brooding face. He thrust his hand into the water and destroyed the image, transforming it into a thousand ripples which spread wider and wider until the pool was calm again, and his reflection whole.

'My loyalties are not so easily scattered as the parts of my likeness,' he said, 'and my loyalty to Pharaoh is proven.'

'Pharaoh is an old man,' said Ka-Maat. 'He is sick and already the mark of Osiris is upon him. The priests who rule Egypt in his name are not of his opinion in all things and not every man who smiles at you is your friend.'

'Osiris will wait a little longer. When Pharaoh sits again in his royal chair I will have much to tell him about the injustice his officials tolerate. He will hear me. Listen, Ka-Maat, when I visit the priest in Goshen, I pass near those brickfields where many of the Hebrew labour, and in such conditions as would shame the lowliest beast. I hear their groans and see their sinews stretched to the utmost limit of endurance. This is work indeed, Ka-Maat. It is work such as you and I will never know, and such that most Egyptians have never even seen. Yet overseers walk among the labourers, with whips in their hands, and urge them with cruel lashes to greater effort – and greater effort is impossible. I have seen men burst their hearts and die, and their companions trample their corpses into the mud because, though their eyes pour tears, they dare not break the chain. There is one Seteki whose own death would be a cause for feasting; he is an overseer of overseers and I think it is from fear of him that the others press so hard. Yet this man eats, laughs and grows fat, and no one sees the evil that he is. And you tell me that *I* am watched!'

'I do but warn you,' replied Ka-Maat. 'This Seteki is nothing to you and can be nothing. The Hebrew will labour in the brickfields and claypits long after he is dead – and after you are dead. It is not given to any one man to change the order of things.'

Perhaps not, thought Ra-Mose, yet there may be one small part of the order that *can* be changed. And he watched Seteki more closely from that day on, and noticed at what times the overseer came and went, and where and when he was most often alone. In one part of his mind he plotted the overseer's death and in another part he told himself that it was but a game he played, as a solitary man will play at chequers with himself, to pass the time.

Yet chance brought the two together, prince and overseer, and there was no going back. It was the moment when dusk has deepened to true night, and Seteki was at leisure and drunk; he did not glance behind him to see if any followed and Ra-Mose slipped after, between shadow and shadow, silent as a hunting cat, his hand on the knife of polished obsidian he carried at his girdle, and his mind obscured save for one thought.

Seteki lurched and stumbled towards the river, stopping

occasionally to scratch his belly and belch. Any man could have taken him then, but the gods, whose ways are secret and unknowable, had brought him to this place to be slain by Ra-Mose and by no other. The distance between them lessened and already the soft splash of leaping frogs and their nocturnal croaking could be heard among the reeds. The river was very near.

Then Ra-Mose sprang and it was quickly done, with no noise beyond one little bubbling cry as the knife went in. It had been easier than killing a calf, he thought. He dragged the corpse through the reeds and left it there, asprawl on the bank, between land and water. Then he stepped back a pace and squatted down to wait.

And soon he came – the scavenging crocodile, more than half of him submerged like a log heavy with water but swifter than the current that bore him, drawn by the smell of blood that had reached him even through his dark, saurian dreams. Ra-Mose saluted him, whispering, 'Feast, my Lord Sebek. Feast and sleep again.' The wide jaws gaped and snapped, the great tail churned the slow, brown water into cream. 'Accept my gift, Lord Sebek, feast and sleep,' said Ra-Mose.

When he awakened the next morning he was like a man who has passed beneath a dreadful shadow and lived to see the sun again. He felt purified, as though he had slain not merely the hated Seteki, but some dark side of himself. He did not go to Goshen that day but lazed on the terraces with his friends who rejoiced to see him so light of heart. He gave no further thought to the blood-stained garment he had dropped so casually on the floor beside his bed and by evening he had almost – though not completely – forgotten Seteki.

When next he passed that way he stood a while to watch the Hebrew at work in the brickfield and wondered how they fared, whether the lash fell less often or less cruelly on their shoulders. Perhaps he would never know, for it was no longer a matter he could discuss with Aaron, whose shrewd eyes could see through a man's most careless utterance to the truth beneath the lie.

It did not occur to him that the overseer might be missed by his own kind, that already questions concerning the man's disappearance were being asked. But in the city men began to whisper, and the whispers grew to a murmur, spreading through the streets and alley-ways until all men spoke of Seteki, saying that he had been murdered. Aye, they said, it was the work of some Hebrew dog – but, said others, what Hebrew leaves his own quarter at night?

Hamor the rebel, idling among the wool-sellers in the market-place, pricked his ears to hear more, but there was no more, nothing beyond the rumour that Prince Ra-Mose should have care, Prince Ra-Mose was being watched. And still it was only rumour. A man, spreading a snowy fleece in the sun, whispered it to another and Hamor caught his arm and asked outright, 'What is that you say?' The man trembled under his hand and said, 'Nothing, I did but speak of the price . . .'

'You are a liar, and the son of a liar. It was a name I heard and no price. Now tell me what was said between you before I slit your lying tongue.'

'Master, these are hard times in which to rear a family . . .'

'They will be harder yet. Now speak.'

Hamor released the man who backed away, rubbing his arm. 'They say Prince Ra-Mose might have something to tell about Seteki's disappearance . . .'

'Prince Ra-Mose and the overseer?' Hamor scoffed. 'Have cattle wings?'

'It is the truth. They say that the Prince's servant found a blood-stained robe the night the overseer was last seen, and it is well known he goes often to Goshen, being enchanted by a Hebrew spell.'

'These are tales for old women,' Hamor said. 'Has the Prince no answer to them?' And the man shook his head. He knew no more than what was said in the market.

Is this Egyptian Prince mad, thought Hamor, that he, alone of all men, has not heard what all men whisper of him? This was a matter that needed wise counsel and Hamor was a proud man, not used to asking advice. It was also a matter that required action, and this was more to his liking. He would go to the Prince and tell him what was said – enmity and distrust set aside – for Ra-Mose himself had crossed the barrier between their two races, had drawn his knife for Israel. Should Hamor ben Kedemah prove a lesser man?

But there was a small crowd outside the Prince's house. A stout Egyptian with a shaven head and sagging belly climbed from a litter, knocked at the outer door and was admitted, not by a servant, but by a member of the royal guard. More officials arrived and went in. The door closed and the crowd waited.

'The servants have all fled away,' said one.

'Aye, and you can be sure they did not go empty-handed,' said another, 'but now Pharaoh's own seal is on the treasure-house and there will be no more pickings . . .'

'Why? What's afoot?' Hamor asked indifferently, and his neighbours turned eagerly to enlighten him. One ancient hung on his arm and spat the news into his face in a reek of wild garlic.

'They say he killed a man – an Egyptian – ill luck to them all!' he wheezed, spittle flying from his mouth. 'They're wait-ing for him now, and not all the service he's done for Pharaoh in his wars is like to help him, and not all his pride nor his handsome looks, nor the anger nor tears of the Princess, his mother. To strike a servant of Pharaoh is the same as striking Pharaoh, I've heard, and there's only one payment for that, my lad.'

He cackled, well pleased with the thought, and Hamor moved away, sickened. Blood spilled in war, or anger, or vengeance or sacrifice – this he could understand – even blood spilled in fear. But the crowd that increased with every moment was making holiday, passing a wineskin from hand to hand, laughing, exchanging jests and ribaldries. If Prince Ra-Mose should, that instant, be brought to execution before his house, these people would gobble the sight with their hungry eyes and make of it a tale to tell their grandchildren. It was unclean.

The Prince must be warned – that much was certain. And if he were not here, at his own house, then surely he would be with Aaron. Hamor freed himself from the expectant crowd and set off to warn the man who had been his enemy.

But Ra-Mose was not with Aaron.

'Then where is he? I must find him, Aaron, and soon!'

'Peace, Hamor. Haste is written on your brow and in your eyes, but before I tell you where the Prince may be found, I must ask your business with him. You understand? Is it in friendship that you seek him?'

'The stars have moved in their courses. My business with Ra-Mose is beyond friendship and enmity but, because he has been a friend to Israel, his freedom, perhaps his life, is in danger. Therefore, Aaron, I must be on my way.'

'You must tell me more.'

Hamor drove the fist of his right hand into the hollowed palm of his left.

'Then I will say to you what all men are saying, that Prince Ra-Mose has slain the overseer, Seteki, and must answer for it before Pharaoh. Now will you tell me where he is and let me go?'

Aaron narrowed his eyes, but said nothing.

Hamor cried, 'The officers of Pharaoh sit in the Prince's house to await his return. The whole city buzzes with the tale.'

'Is this a rumour that began in the market-place?' Aaron asked him. 'Words whispered between the lip and the ear change in the telling, and change again. Who can say truly why Pharaoh has sent to the Prince's house? But, Hamor, are they not kinsmen? There may be other matters between them than the one you speak of. And who can say truly that the overseer is dead?'

'*I* can,' said Hamor, and he shivered so that the teeth chattered in his head. 'With my own eyes I saw Prince Ra-Mose give Seteki to the crocodile.'

Aaron looked up sharply, his hand raised as though to strike the younger man. 'Was it you who betrayed him?' he demanded.

'It was not. I have not trusted him as you have trusted him but it was not my tongue that broke the silence. Seteki is dead. I would have been well content to leave him so.'

Aaron saw the truth in his eyes and let his hand fall. 'He is with your brother Ishvi,' he said. 'May El go with you and guard you both.'

But when Hamor reached Ishvi's dwelling-place Ra-Mose had already left. 'Not long since,' said Ishvi, surprised by the urgency in his brother's voice. 'He brought a gift of wine and figs for Laban's family; we talked a while and then he went his way. We are simple people – what should keep him here?'

'How long? How long?' Hamor's voice was harsh with impatience. 'I have not come to juggle words with you, Ishvi. Which way went he and how long ago?'

'Towards the city,' said Ishvi, though Leah frowned and shook her head at him. 'And as to the time – that which exists between a child's cry in the night and the mother's rising. Hardly longer.'

Ah, that was good. The Prince would have taken the wide road as he always did, but by narrow ways between the backs of houses Hamor might yet head him off before he reached the city. Night would cloak their meeting and it were better so, since death and flight were dark words, not to be spoken by sunlight or firelight or in the presence of people not intimately concerned. Few were abroad at that hour and only Zorah saw him pass. He shook his head, thinking, 'That Hamor! There is no peace in him!'

Neither was there peace in the Prince's heart as he took the road that was now so familiar to him. However many times he visited the Hebrew settlement in Goshen he could never accustom himself to the poverty he saw everywhere, his very heart shrank from it. Yet this poverty *they* called wealth, thanking their gods for a few thin cattle, a few starveling goats and sharing their precious little. One half of their plenty for the poor! And such a plenty! His own slaves were fatter and more wasteful. And what a pride they had, these Israelites, these free wretches who would have known greater bodily comfort in true slavery. Their pride was as great as Pharaoh's . . . it was beyond reason . . .

From between two houses a man stepped, barring his way. This was a district of mean hovels; neither properly in the Hebrew quarter nor in the city, it was the haunt of outcasts of both races and no honest man walked here by night, he knew. But Prince Ra-Mose had no fear of thieves. Rather, let them fear him, for his gold was not to be easily had. Smiling, he took the man by the neck and drew him nearer, choking the words he might have said.

'Thief,' said Ra-Mose, softly, 'better for you had you been content to have starved with your brethren.'

55

His hands tightened their grip. His will was something apart. It did not even say to him *Kill* as it had said that other night. This was a matter between his hands and the throat they bruised; it did not even concern him as a man who thought, who lived and felt compassion. It did not even concern him as a man who felt anger. His mind, separate, said that death, given by one man to another, needed some part of all these things – thought, pity and anger – but his hands had a need his mind could not deny.

His thumbs moved, searching out the place where the breath rasped. The man suddenly relaxed, his weight a shock that made Ra-Mose stumble. It was but an instant in time – but it was enough. A knee thrust him back and, simultaneously, two hands forced his own apart. A voice he knew said, 'Fool, would you kill me as you killed the Egyptian?'

'Hamor!' Then, suspicion gnawing within his skull, 'What do you know of that?'

'All Egypt speaks of it. Hear me, Prince, and if you have ever in your life trusted any man, trust now an Israelite. The servants of Pharaoh are in your house. Even at this moment they may be looking for you in the city; when they do not find you they will search among the dwellings of my people, and they must not find you there. Our lives are heavy enough without that. So, Ra-Mose, go now, go quickly and may the protection of all the gods be with you, your gods and mine . . . because of what you did for Israel's sake.'

'Where shall I go?' said Ra-Mose. 'What house will shelter me when I leave behind me a bloody trail to lead my enemies?'

'No house in Goshen,' Hamor answered. 'But leave Egypt. Go to the east and southward into Midian, to the tents of the nomad peoples, the Kenites. We have some kinship with them, for they too are sons of Abram, but they are free men, paying no tribute. They will judge you as a man like themselves. And go now!'

Still Ra-Mose hesitated. 'I would reward you for this service,' he said, 'but there is no treasure on earth that, weighed against a man's life, will turn the balance. At least let me pay you for the marks my fingers put upon your neck . . .' And he made to tear the golden scarab from his breast, but Hamor drew back.

'I want no Egyptian bauble.' He spat contemptuously in the scuffled dust. 'Should a son of the Bull stoop to wear a dung-beetle to remind him of a duty done? Keep it, man. Gold may not buy life between free men, but it will buy meat and water. Those things you will need before long.'

So Ra-Mose turned away, setting his back to the city that had once honoured him above all others, and all those things in it that he had loved – friends and servants and position. He had made of himself an exile and for no reason that his mind could encompass. Egypt was one thing and Israel another. For a time he had held them together in one hand, but Egypt he had learned to despise for Israel's sake, and now Israel rejected his gift, the only thing left to him of all his wealth. But Hamor came after him in the shadows and put his own striped robe about the Prince's shoulders.

'It will let you pass for one of us,' he said, 'but keep away from the traders' road for you do not walk like an Israelite.'

6

For a little while the Prince was missed and then he was forgotten. The people were busy with other things. The Prince
had amused himself, they thought, and what more natural for
a young man with time on his hands? The amusement had
palled and he was seen no more. Ah yes! There had been soldiers asking questions, but they did not stay; it was a little
excitement to spice the days, but nothing came of it. Enough is
enough. There were still the cows to keep and the goats to
watch, marriages and deaths, celebration and mourning – and
always the service to Pharaoh. The children missed him longest
for he had had time for them when their own fathers were too
weary or too troubled for play; he had entertained them with
his stories about magicians and gods, and about the great battles he had fought. The youngest had climbed on his knees and
tugged at the shining, yellow beetle that hung from a chain
about his neck – but those had been the best days; sometimes he
had not noticed them at all. For a few days they played at being
Prince Ra-Mose of Egypt, pursuing the enemy into strange
lands – and then they, too, forgot him.

Prince Ra-Mose knew the desert. He knew how to save his
strength in the heat of the day and how to make fire when the
night grew cold. In the distance he saw the caravans go by,
long strings of mules and oxen, laden with merchandise from
the east, from the mysterious lands beyond the hills of Canaan;
he saw troops of soldiers pass on the horizon, their spear-heads
catching the light in a golden dazzle, and he wondered if they
were seeking him. But they did not turn aside; they went on

southwards to guard the frontier that he, Prince Ra-Mose, had made. Once he encountered a party of slaves from the copper mines of Sinai, driven by Egyptian slave-masters, and, greatly daring, had asked the distance to the next *wadi* that he might fill his water-bottle. They were rough and ignorant men; it did not occur to them to wonder how he spoke their tongue with such ease or why he travelled alone with no sheep or goats to give a purpose to his wandering. They gave him water and bread and in return he told them the news of the city.

After many days and nights of travelling through country that grew rougher and wilder he came at last to the place where men dwelt in black tents and counted their wealth in flocks, the high pastures of the Midianites. There he sat down near a spring of fresh water that gushed from the rock above the green slopes where the tents clustered, and thought how he should best approach these desert princes – whether to go to them as an exiled nobleman seeking sanctuary or simply as a man, stripped to the husk, having two hands that could work and a belly that hungered. He would go down at evening when their fires would sprinkle the valley with red stars, the smoke savoury with the smell of roasting mutton – but now the sun hung in the sky midway between its noon height and its sinking. He need not decide at once.

Seven young women, bearing pitchers on their shoulders, climbed the well-trodden path towards the spring, their voices calling across the small distance between them and their laughter as musical as the songs of birds. When they had almost reached the spring and were pausing to draw breath after the climb, some shepherds came whooping down from above, pushing and jostling each other to reach the water first, and bringing sheep with them to muddy the clear stream. The first of the maidens had already stooped to fill her vessel when the sheep came tumbling down to their guardians' shouts and she was thrust aside so that she almost fell. The leader of the shepherds called to her that she should have a care but none of them made any move to help her and the sheep plunged everywhere, bleating and scattering the water.

The sight angered Ra-Mose and he leapt down from the rock, brandishing his staff and, though he was but one man and the shepherds were several, they stood back, humble before his fierceness and the sound of authority in his voice.

'Carrion dogs!' he said. 'Beasts and eaters of offal, by what right do you pollute this stream while others wait?'

'It is the right of all men to use this water which belongs to no man,' answered one, sullenly.

'To use it with decency and thanksgiving,' said Ra-Mose, and he went among the sheep, slapping their woolly rumps and driving them back to the grass.

'Fill your pitchers,' he told the maidens. 'It is more fitting that beauty be served before brutishness.'

Quickly they did as he bade them and went away down the path while Ra-Mose watched them go. Then he turned his back and let the shepherds go to the well, and the sheep with them, and other people came and went and the sun dropped lower in the sky.

At the moment when its lower rim just touched the edge of the land, turning the sky to bronze, he was hailed by a youth who bowed and said, 'Stranger, I am bid to bring you to Jethro's tent.' Ra-Mose marked his proud carriage and the curious mark tattooed above his brow and knew that this lad, in his way, was as nobly descended as himself. 'I will go with you,' he said, and rose to his feet.

Jethro stood at the entrance to his tent, a tall old man, his face ravaged and furrowed by time but his eyes still bright and his back as straight as many a younger man's. He wore the loose robe of striped wool that all his people wore but, knotted into his headband were the horns of a bull, distinguishing him as priest and leader of the tribe, as did the red-daubed aurochs-skull raised on a post before his tent. Ra-Mose abased himself before this symbol of the god.

'I am your slave and the servant of your slaves,' he said, but his voice had little humility in it. Jethro drew him to his feet and answered, 'My tent is unworthy, but it is yours,' in a voice that was full of pride.

Within the tent the daughters of Jethro brought lamps to drive away the darkness, herb-scented water to cleanse the guest's hands, and food and drink in abundance, such a feast as men dream of in the desert.

The two men ate in silence; Jethro, as custom demanded, tasting of each dish before it was set before the Prince. It was a leisurely meal, for the old man would not show, by any display of haste, that his curiosity was roused and Ra-Mose, in his turn, would not insult such noble hospitality by an appearance of greed. But at last it was done and Jethro leaned back against the great pillows of woven goat-hair; it was the time for speech.

'I am an old man,' he prompted, 'but I have my sight still. My eyes tell me that, beneath the garment you wear, you are an Egyptian. Therefore it seems the garment is a borrowed one – and my mind asks why. You were hungry and there was so great a weariness in your limbs you could travel no further – yet you took the part of the daughters of Midian when they were pushed aside from the well by those wild young shepherds from the hills. My curiosity, I know, exceeds the bounds of courtesy and you have a right to be silent. Yet I also have the right to ask, for what shall a man think of a stranger who, by his voice and manner, proclaims himself of high birth, when that stranger comes, footsore and exhausted, clad in a borrowed robe . . . and he an Egyptian?'

'Egyptians are but men,' Ra-Mose answered, carefully, 'as Kenites are men, and Hurrites, and Hittites. Whatever garment a man wears he knows the same passions as other men – and sometimes they lead him into trouble, as mine have led me. It is true that I have fled my country in a borrowed robe.'

'I think there was death in it,' said Jethro, 'for a man does not travel so far over a matter of taxes.'

'There was death in it. I will not hide it from you. And the man I killed is better dead. An Israelite gave me the coat from his back that I might pass unrecognised, and it was that same Israelite who directed me to seek shelter among your tents. If my Egyptian blood affronts you I will go, but first let me ask you this – what man is different from another, save in the manner of his dwelling?'

'And in his gods,' Jethro reminded him. 'In Egypt are many gods, they tell me, lords of life and death and each given worship according to his nature. This is strange to us who make but one sacrifice and that to one god. Tell me, Egyptian, is it true that in your land all life is but a preparation for death?'

'Is this not true in every land? Surely we must all die, priest of Midian.'

'Yet in Egypt, I have heard, are palaces built to house the dead who lie, preserved from corruption, until the end of time. It is a dark thought.'

'That is our way in Egypt,' Ra-Mose admitted. 'For how otherwise shall a man be joined with Osiris and live again? The days of our breath are short indeed – but who can measure the life span of those six imponderable parts our priests know of, the essential and eternal parts of man? Where would the *ka* fly once his habitation had fallen into dust?'

Jethro shrugged. 'As I have said, a man's gods set him apart from other men. One tribe may dwell in the mountains, another by the shore and they may speak with the same tongue, but let one tribe worship life and the other death, and there will be blood spilled between them.'

'Then tell me of your god,' said Ra-Mose, 'that I may not unwittingly offend him, for I am a stranger in a strange country, your guest and your god's guest. By the aurochs-skull at your tent opening and the horns you wear above your brow I would say that you follow Bull-El as do the Israelites in the land of Goshen. Would I say truly?'

'Not Bull-El, stranger, but Yahweh, the wild ox, lord of storms. His is the voice heard in the hilltops; he stamps his foot and the ground quakes. It was he who set the mark on the head of our first-father, Cain, when he slew his brother in the fields. Yahweh is not appeased by grain-offering such as they make to Bull-El in Goshen.'

Ra-Mose lowered his eyes, acknowledging his error. 'Tell me more about Cain, your first-father, and why he shed his brother's blood, that in this way I may come to the heart of your god and offend him not.'

Jethro clapped his hands and one of his daughters brought a pitcher of date wine which she set by his hand, and another brought sweetmeats to offer her father's guest.

'Are they not fair?' asked Jethro. 'Seven daughters have I, yet no son to be priest after me, for the god has not breathed on Hobab. My son will be a shepherd.'

'They are fair indeed,' said Ra-Mose, and he knew well what was in Jethro's mind. 'But tell me about your first-father, Cain, and the mark your tribe bears to this day.'

The priest nodded, satisfied that the stranger was not to be diverted so easily. 'Thus it is told among my people,' he said, 'from generation to generation, since the beginning of all things. The name of the first man was Adam, for he was created from the red dust of the earth, and Cain was his first-born son. In those days he was a tiller of the soil; he planted seeds in the ground and the rain fell upon them and the sun warmed them so that they grew tall. Then the plants bowed before Cain's sickle as he, himself, bowed before Yahweh – and the first sheaf to be garnered from every harvest he offered to the god. But Cain had a brother, whose name was Abel, and he was a keeper of flocks; these two strove together for Yahweh's favour, the one with his gift of grain and the first-fruits of the ground, the other with the first-born of his lambs. And Yahweh accepted the blood-offering so that Abel prospered and his herds multiplied – while Cain stooped over the thin soil, labouring from one harvest to the next.

'Then it was that Abel taunted Cain, telling him that his sheep would eat up all the land, cropping it to the rock beneath. And Cain looked up and saw the sun like fire in a sky of bronze and it seemed to him that Yahweh spoke from within the fire, saying, "It is good that your brother Abel pours out blood upon the ground, for blood is life. If my rain waters your corn, what do you give me that is not my own?"

'Cain gave a great cry and sprang upon his brother. His sickle was in his hand and, when he looked again, Abel was dead and the earth drank his blood, even as it had the blood of Abel's lambs. Seeing that, Cain ran from the place and hid himself from the wrath of Yahweh. But the voice pursued him, asking, "Cain, where is your brother?" And Cain lay shivering in his tent and said, "Am I my brother's keeper? Surely he is with his flocks on the hillside." Even as he spoke, he heard the blood of Abel crying aloud from the ground so that, weeping, he fled away into the wilderness where Yahweh sought him out and put the brand on his forehead so that all generations of men should stay their hands from slaying him who had shed his brother's blood.'

Ra-Mose considered a while without speaking. Then he said, very quietly as though he did but think aloud, 'The god chose the sacrifice and the place of offering. Your first-father was but the tool . . .'

'When the Bull stamps, the earth shakes and a man must stand by whatever means he can find. Once Cain had learned his god's desire he did not look back. He asked no further crop of the earth lest it should bear armed men, springing like spears of corn from his brother's spilth. And Yahweh gave all the flocks into his hand and led him into the hills.'

As Ra-Mose did not answer at once, Jethro added, 'Perhaps the god has also set his mark on you, Egyptian,' and Ra-Mose remembered the haste and flurry of the crocodile's feast, and shuddered.

'That we shall know in time,' said Jethro. 'But for what you have done this day, we owe you thanks. Therefore accept the shelter of these black tents and the brotherhood of these, my people, for as long as you care to dwell with us. Egypt will not trouble you here. But by what name shall we call you? How are you called among your own people?'

'I am called Ra-Mose.'

'Ra-Mose.' Jethro tried the name. 'Ra-Mose! That has too much of an Egyptian sound. Should those of our tribesmen who water their flocks on the furthest borders of the waste be questioned, such a name on their tongues might bring dangers upon us all. Ra-Mose! Let your name now be Moses, stranger. Moses, be welcome to our tents, and a stranger no more.'

7

Thus it came about that Ra-Mose became Moses and dwelt as a guest in Jethro's tent, speaking the language of Midian and eating the food that was set before him, rich stews of mutton spiced with coriander, quails skinned and spitted, roasted above the red embers of the fire, followed by great draughts of the sweet and heady date wine.

Sitting at Jethro's side he learned the tribe's history, as he had learned that of the Tribes of Joseph from Aaron so many moons before. He learned how many of the descendants of Cain had become workers in metal, first making rings and small ornaments from the copper they found in the mountains of Sinai, hammering it and heating it and hammering again until they had developed within themselves an extra sense that warned them of the exact moment when the metal must be heated yet again lest it crack from the stress of beating. He learned how traders from the sea-coast brought tin-ore to the tribe, and how the coppersmiths turned to the making of bronze, weapons as well as ornaments.

'Our people travel far in the practice of their craft,' said Jethro. 'Wherever the earth shows veins of metal there will a Kenite smith strike fire and lay out his tools. Even in the cities you will find them, working in gold and silver brought from distant places, and fulfilling the prophecy that the sons of Cain would be dwellers in cities . . .'

And again and again the priest would mark how Moses' eyes followed Zipporah, the dearest of his daughters, as she went about her work, and his own eyes narrowed in speculation. Then he would say, 'The priesthood of Midian hangs at the girdles of my daughters, for Hobab, my son, is of the land only. See how tenderly he comforts a ewe in travail, and rears her lambs. He can find pasture and water where even a goat will pass it by; he has the art of sweetening bitter streams and of distilling medicines from the juice of wild plants, the cactus and myrrh and camphor that grow in the waste places. But more than these things are required of a priest.'

Moses, watching Zipporah, would nod but his mind was absent. It was nothing to him whether Hobab was priest or shepherd, whether his hands were shaped to the crook or the sacrificial knife. But Zipporah was like the moon riding the night-sky above the Nile; she was like a reed bowing before the wind, like a lotus opening its waxy petals on the surface of a shadowy pool. And Jethro saw how the young man's thoughts had sped away and he smiled, stroking the white fleece of his beard.

The long season of summer drought dragged on. Moses' own beard grew black and lustrous and his eyes changed, focussed so often on the distance where the sheep ranged afar that they became like the eyes of caged beasts that seem to rest on nothing nearer than the horizon. His skin darkened under the perpetual sun and in a while no man could have told that he was not a Midianite; the tribe had swallowed him.

Then, without warning, there was thunder in the air and in the mountains the storm-god raged and bellowed in his bull voice. Soon the rain would come and there would be sweet grass springing between the acacias and aromatic bushes on the slopes. Already the white ewe and the black ram had been chosen for the thank-offering, their hooves polished and the horns of the ram gilded.

Moses looked out from Jethro's tent and saw the whole land stained with red. In his belly he felt the bull stir and he lowered his head and struck the ground with the ball of his foot. There was an ache in his temples like that a beast might feel, cutting horns, and the weight as of a yoke on his shoulders. The god thundered in the mountain and Moses, restless as a stalled ox, bellowed his reply.

Behind him Jethro said, 'The earth awaits the bridegroom,' and he took Moses by the hand and led him into the innermost place of the tent where Zipporah waited with her veil aside and her dark hair tumbled about her shoulders.

Nine moons waxed and waned and Zipporah went to the birth-stool, exulting. Outside the tent her sisters waited for the child's first cry; the midwife parted the heavy folds and gave the news they must carry to the father and they ran, their very feet rejoicing, to Moses where he walked with Jethro under the stars.

'A bull calf is born,' they said. 'Come.'

The old women had washed and swaddled the child in readiness, and Zipporah lay at peace behind a curtain in the tent for it was not fitting that she should be seen by her husband at that time.

It was a very small bull calf, he thought, remembering the thunders of its begetting. Surely such a little helpless thing would never survive to lead a tribe. He put his hand against his son's cheek and the child turned its head to nuzzle his finger with its damp mouth. Jethro touched the child's lips with date juice and wild honey; his daughters strewed herbs across the threshold and kindled seven lamps to cast out whatever demons the dark might shelter. The eldest twisted a scarlet thread amongst the swaddling bands . . .

'Name him,' Jethro commanded, 'for already the evil ones, the dwellers in the waste, gather without the tent. The *Emmim* are crouching at the door. Name your boy. Give him the protection of his name.'

Moses' heart was heavy as he looked at his first-born son. Born into exile, lulled to sleep by the cradle-songs of an alien

68

race – how much of Egypt, he wondered, flowed in those branching veins.

'He shall be called Gershom,' he said, 'which means stranger, for I have been a sojourner in a strange land.'

And behind the curtain Zipporah heard the bitterness in his voice and wept. The child was named and the *Emmim* banished to the far places – that much was good. Yet the child was set apart by such a name, a stranger not only to his father but to his tribe.

'Not so,' said Jethro, later, to comfort her. 'This little bull calf is for Midian, I promise you. Perhaps my son-in-law, the Egyptian, is one of those who fear their sons; there are such men . . .'

'It is not that,' cried Zipporah. 'My husband fears nothing. But it is Egypt he longs for still – the gardens and cool houses, the pools and terraces, those cold, death-dwelling gods. Perhaps even the tombs are a part of his desire. Whatever *that* may be, it is not here in the tents of Midian, or in the voice of the storm-god. And it is not in my arms, my father.'

Jethro frowned and answered, 'These are fancies. You have come lately from a heavy task and at such times many women feel the pull of grief, weeping when they should rejoice. There is no such division between your heart and your husband's heart as you imagine. Would I, a priest, have married my daughter to a stranger? The god willed it, Zipporah. The tribe accepted him. Be at peace.'

But after that he watched Moses carefully and trusted him less.

When Gershom was eight days old he was taken from the House of Birth and given to his father to be circumcised according to the old law.

'Our fathers gave the first fruits,' Jethro told Moses, 'the first of the flocks, the first of the herds and, in those ancient days, the first of their sons also. Now we redeem our sons and make but a token offering. It is a small thing, Moses, yet the god accepts it, and blesses our children with health and long life.'

'This child's veins contain Egyptian blood as well as Kenite,' said Moses, 'and though the sacrifice is not unknown in my country, it is not common in my house. Also I do not consider it fitting that such mingled blood should flow in honour of your desert god.'

'It is most fitting,' Jethro replied, his voice low but with anger in it, 'for this child was got on the daughter of a priest, by the god's favour. The night this son of yours was conceived the skies opened and the land ran with rain.'

'Then you perform the rite,' said Moses, and his voice too was angry. 'If the god desires it, so let it be. But I will not touch this sickle to my son's flesh.'

He knew as he turned his back on his father-in-law that he was making much of a little thing but he hardened his heart and let his generosity wither. He had accepted so much from this tribe, too much. Even his wife and child, his life itself, he owed to Jethro and to Jethro's people; it made him churlish, so that he could give nothing in return. Also there was fear at the back of his mind, reminding him that once before he had taken a stone knife and spilled Egyptian blood.

Jethro took the sickle and dedicated the child to Yahweh as it had to be, but now the division of mistrust between himself and Moses was no longer quite beneath the surface. It showed in all their dealings with each other.

When Zipporah bore her second son, Eliazar, Jethro again performed the rite, and that time Moses was not there to see it done.

8

In Egypt Pharaoh, the living Osiris, reached the end of his days and went to join the dead Osiris in the underworld. His body that had housed the incarnate god now lay empty beneath the embalmers' hands; heart, lungs, liver and intestines sealed in canopic jars, the lids carved in the semblance of the heads of the four sons of Horus, man-headed Mesti, ape-headed Hapi, Tuamutef the jackal, and the falcon Quebhsenuf, guardians of north, south, east and west. Pharaoh, who had lived and breathed, wielding such power over life and death as no other man could dream of, lay shrouded in linen bands, his dead face hidden beneath a golden mask. His painted coffin awaited him.

In the tomb attendants arranged the furniture that would surround him now until the end of time – chairs and beds, all carved and gilded; chariots; chests of black wood and white wood, painted with scenes of hunting and warfare; a fleet of boats with their prows all pointing to the west – and, most precious symbol of the resurrection, a narrow box having within it a frame shaped in the likeness of the mummified Osiris, filled with rich Nile mud and sown with corn-seed that would germinate there in the eternal darkness until it sprouted a new Osiris of golden corn. And there were humbler offerings too, the little wooden *ushabti* figures that represented all the trades known to man, set there to serve dead Pharaoh in the otherworld. And on the walls were depicted the offering of loaves and geese and beer, provisions such as the *ka* would need for food and drink.

Then all was ready for the last great journey. The chain of

mourners moved in slow procession along the western bank of the Nile. At the tomb the sarcophagus was met by a priest who, wearing the jackal-mask of the god Anubis, was to perform the ceremony of the Opening of the Mouth, that the dead man might speak again and eat and drink.

First the priest took in his hands two magical instruments of precious meteoric iron and with them touched the mouth and eyes of the mummy, saying: 'Thy mouth was closed but I have set it in order, thy mouth and teeth I have set in order. I open for thee thy mouth; I open for thee thy eyes. With these instruments, the tools of Anubis, I have opened thy mouth as the mouths of the gods were opened. Horus, open the mouth! Horus, open the mouth!

'The dead shall walk and speak, the body shall be with the gods in the Great House of Annu, and he shall receive the crown from Horus, the lord of mankind.'

The people, watching, gave a great sigh.

Next the priest took the *ur hekau*, a piece of wood, curved and twisting and with one end carved in the shape of a ram's head wearing the cobra circlet, the *uraeus*, and again touched the mummy's mouth and eyes. Four times he touched them with the *ur hekau*. Now Pharaoh was endowed with the words of power and the ability to utter them. But it was not yet over. Pharaoh's son, who succeeded him, then touched the eyes and mouth of his dead father with a little bag containing red stones and carnelian. Ceremonially and with proper respect, food was offered. The priest waved an ostrich feather four times before the unseeing face.

At last the coffin was lowered to its final resting place and the entrance to the tomb sealed. The dead Pharaoh slept with Osiris and the living Pharaoh, a slender cold-eyed boy, was carried in his great litter back to the palace.

For the children of Israel nothing was changed. The sun and the moon moved in their measured paces across the sky and the seasons followed each other, seed-time and harvest, sacrifice and feast. The old died and were buried in caves at the edge of the waste; the young married and bore children and toiled in the fields, trudging behind the patient oxen or themselves yoked to the plough. And to the west of the city others sweated, raising stone upon stone, as the young Pharaoh, not yet a man, ordered the building of the tomb that was to be his own.

At this time Zorah died, his patient heart ceasing to beat one night and his spirit flying away into the otherworld as easily as a dove flies from the hand. There had been no sickness, no expectation of death, and the shock to Rebekkah was great. For so many years she had scolded and harried him, contesting his every action and yet loving him with a warmth her words belied – now she was alone. For just one year she stayed but, without Zorah, the world was meaningless to her. Leah mourned first one and then the other; after that Ishvi and her children, Naboth and Zillah, occupied all her life. Micael visited them often and Ishvi, in his ever-waxing prosperity, was able now and then to help his unlucky brother; Leah sat with Micael's wife in her labour and later the little ones played together. Hamor they rarely saw.

Ishvi had, in filial duty, offered a home to old Kedemah, but it had been refused. Micael, he said, was the eldest son, it was for him to provide shelter for his father's age. Nevertheless the old man sat most nights by Ishvi's fire and ate whatever food Leah prepared, grumbling at the quality but his hand returning often to the dish. The years had not touched Kedemah in any way. The children were a little in awe of him and his presence constrained them. To Naboth he seemed as ancient as Grandfather Abram and he confused the two in his mind. Sitting at

73

Kedemah's feet he tried to imagine this meagre old man walking with the Great Spirit and making bargains with him; that Kedemah could bargain well he knew, and wondered how it had happened that Israel should have got the worst of it. He tried to discuss the subject with his sister but Zillah was still too young to have any sense. She did not care about Grandfather Abram's glorious past; she only knew she was afraid of *this* old man and that, as Naboth thought, for the silliest reason – because of his deafness. She decided he must dislike her very much to ignore everything she said to him and, if he disliked her as much as that, then he might do anything – he might even curse her.

On the whole the evenings were not comfortable and Leah was heartily thankful that her husband's father did not live with them entirely. Once, when they were alone together, she said to Ishvi, 'Promise me something. Promise that when you are old and your beard is white, you will not be too much like old Kedemah.'

And Ishvi promised. 'Not every son is cut to his father's pattern, my love.'

'Ah, not one of his sons is like him *now*,' said Leah, 'but the years that will whittle the flesh from your bones, and dull your sight and deaden your hearing – may they not also pare away the generosity from your heart?'

'I am not like my father,' Ishvi vowed. 'Though a thousand years should weigh down my limbs, I will never change towards you. We shall be old together and sit hand in hand at Naboth's fire. It will be good, I promise you.'

And Leah wept and said she was a foolish woman; she would love Kedemah for Ishvi's sake. Perhaps there was an excuse for her foolishness for, not many months after that, there was a new child, another boy, whom they called Naaman. And this one Kedemah loved, more indeed than he had ever

74

loved his own sons. It made him gentle and less inclined to find fault with everything about him. Also the little one seemed to love him and never cried when he was near.

9

The years ran on and Moses remained with the Kenite tribes of Midian, moving when they moved, following the flocks from pasture to pasture, watching his stranger son, his first-born, grow from a baby to a boy, straight-backed and shaggy. The black tents of Jethro were his home, the shepherds and coppersmiths his brothers. There was scarcely anything of the Egyptian to be seen in him now, and Zipporah was glad.

Yet there were still times when he thought of Egypt. There were days when his eyes wearied of looking at the red desert that was channelled with green where springs burst from the rock, pouring their water down precipitate gullies, to tumble and race for as long as the god willed. Such a spring might water a valley during the time it takes for a boy to age into a man and get boys of his own – and then, as suddenly as it came, dry up. When that happened, the tribes must move. It was a harsh and obstinate land and only a harsh and obstinate people could dwell in it. But Egypt – ah! Moses thought longingly of the great, slow-moving river with its wide flood-plains and fronded palms, of the fish he had speared there, stooping from a raft of papyrus reeds lashed together; of the birds, rosy-legged pelicans, hoopoes, zic-zacs and the gentle ibis; of the swarming city-streets with their bustle and noise and the gods carried in procession ... Then he would try to forget his longing in fierce play with his boys, unsettling them until Zipporah declared he was as unmanageable as they.

There were other days when thunder flickered in the sky and the god's voice bellowed, echoing among the peaks, and then his melancholy left him. Seeking the bull, he would crouch, motionless in the sun's full glare, from first light to the stars' showing, tormented at noon, shaking with thirst by nightfall, but all his strength and will directed to one purpose – to awake the bull, to feel the bull's hot breath, redolent of grass, on his skin, to touch the wide horns and gleaming shoulders. Deep in his being, below the level of thought, lay the boast, *I will harness this bull of Midian and between us we will plough such a furrow that will make the whole earth wonder.*

On one such day as this, Moses left his flocks in Hobab's charge and climbed towards the crags that stood like brooding giants against the sky. At last he reached a place of rocks and stones, twisted bushes and stunted trees. The sun was a disc of molten metal in the white vault of the heavens and the very air seemed to tremble above the ground. This was the heart of the furnace that was Midian, the secret place where the god walked in fire. The very thorns burned in the heat, flames ran along their branches and licked the sparse leaves – yet not a single bush was consumed. Moses, who had once been Ra-Mose of Egypt, beloved of Isis, cast aside his sandals and went bare-footed as any wandering shepherd to meet what would come, winged demon or trampling bull.

Yet it was neither of these that came to him but a voice – a voice like the first low rumble of thunder with the crackle of lightning in it, a voice that came from all around, from the twin peaks of Horeb that towered above, from the burning trees – from within his own skull. And it spoke his name, the name that the Kenites had given him: 'Moses! Moses!'

'I hear,' answered Moses, his own voice no louder than a whisper. He moistened his scorched lips with his tongue and said again, 'I hear!'

And the voice said, 'Know that I am the god of Jethro!' and again, 'I am also El-Shaddai of the mountains, he who brought

Abram out of Chaldea and turned aside his knife from the flesh of his son Isaac in the land of Moriah. It was I that wrestled with Ya'cob on that mount men call Peni'el. Do *you* dare to look on my face, little prince of Egypt?'

'I dare not,' said Moses, and covered his eyes with the sleeve of his robe. It seemed then as though the god laughed, for the ground trembled and shook under Moses' feet and great cracks appeared in it.

The voice continued: 'I have not forgotten Israel. I know that my people groan beneath the weight of Egypt; I have seen their hardship and heard their lamentations. And now, as I promised, I will bring them out from Pharaoh's dominion and set them down in Canaan to be lords of that land . . .' Again the laughter rumbled around the hilltops. 'And you, Egyptian, shall lead them.'

Moses flung himself down on the red earth and cried, 'That cannot be!' Then, in a quieter voice, he said, 'Should I set but one foot across the border into Egypt I would be killed for that which I did to one of Pharaoh's servants, though it was long ago.' And he thought, 'Also what Israelite would follow me – a man of a hated race?'

But the voice spoke again, soft and caressing as a moth's wing: 'I will be with you. Say to them that the god of their fathers has sent you.'

Now it was Moses' turn to laugh. 'The god of their fathers?' he scoffed. 'I tell you, in the land of Goshen are men who worship Bull-El, the strong and plodding ox who fertilises the ground with his dung and treads his enemies into the mud, and there are others who bow to the Lady and some call her Inanna-Ishtar but she is also Astarte and Ashera and Anat. And what of Aleyan-Baal, bringer of rain, lord over the furrows of the field? What of Anu and Enlil? What of Lahar the cattle-god, and Ashnan the grain-goddess? Israel has many gods,

Great One. What then do I answer the people when they say, "Prince Moses, in what name does the god send you?" '

There was anger in the god's voice when he answered, and lightning forked from the sky. 'Say to them that *Yahweh* sent you, the god who is what he is and will be what he will be! In that name will they remember the god of Abram, and they will hearken to your words.'

Then the clouds gathered and blotted out the sun; the world grew dark and the rocks and trees assumed strange shapes like the heads of horned beasts and beasts with wings. But a moment since, the Egyptian had been ringed about with fire, now darkness circled him and, in place of the thunder's bellowing, there was a hissing silence. Turning, he stumbled and dropped his shepherds' staff which, when he put out his hand to take it up again, became a serpent that spat at him with its flickering tongue. But in Egypt, as a boy, he had learned the trick of handling snakes and memory came to his aid. 'Not that way, Ra-Mose, but this,' he said aloud, and put out his hand again. Yet, after all, it was no serpent but his staff.

That night Moses said to Jethro, 'The time has come when I must return to Egypt. These hills have made a wall of safety round me – but a man cannot live for ever behind a shield.'

Jethro looked sharply at him. 'Why not? Are not my people your people now? Did I not give you my daughter Zipporah, my white ewe lamb, to be your wife? Your sons are my grandsons, Moses, this land is your land.'

'There is another need,' said Moses.

'There cannot be! Is it that your gods call you? That cannot be! You have served my god at his place of worship; I have redeemed your sons from him according to his law. This is your tribe . . .'

'There are kindred tribes in Egypt, Jethro, and they are in

79

bondage while we are free. Surely the god made a covenant between himself and your forefather, Abram, that all the land of Canaan should be his, and his sons' also, and that his seed should be numbered as the stars in the heavens? Yet twelve tribes remain in Egypt and may not leave.'

'And what is this to you?'

'I have heard too that the god made the same promise to Ya'cob on Mount Peni'el, at the place men still call Beth-El. Yet twelve tribes remain in Egypt.'

'You must be more plain with me,' said Jethro. 'You cannot mean to share the hardships of the tribes in Egypt. No man willingly puts his shoulders beneath the yoke.'

Then Moses went on his knees before Jethro and pleaded with him. 'You have said that your people are my people, that we are flesh of one flesh. How is it that *I* feel the heaviness of their burden, and you do not?'

Jethro made an impatient gesture with his hands. 'Was it not Joseph who took the people – his brothers and his brothers' wives and their children – into Egypt for the sake of Egyptian corn when the land was dry and the children cried for bread? They went in free men, Moses.'

'When the god walked between the carcasses of Abram's sacrifice in token of his pact with him, he made no separation between this one and that of Abram's seed, that this man should be free and that enslaved. And the Joseph who served the Pharaoh of his day was the son of Ya'cob, and Ya'cob was the son of Isaac, and Isaac was the son of Abram.'

Jethro shrugged, yet what Moses said he could not dismiss, and he could not close his ears to the words, nor shut from his eyes the sight of Moses' dark face so near his own. 'And what is that to me?' he said.

'This – that in his age Abram took to himself another wife. Her name was Keturah and she bore six sons. One of these sons

80

was Midian and the father of your tribe. We are indeed one people, Jethro. And for *this* reason I will return to Egypt and cast in my lot with my brothers there.'

'Go then,' said Jethro, with a gesture of renunciation, 'but Zipporah and her sons will remain here, for have I not said that Gershom shall follow me in the priesthood of the tribe? If you go, you go alone, Egyptian!'

And he would say no more.

Nevertheless when Moses left the black tents behind him the next day, Zipporah went with him, carrying Eliazar in a sling from her shoulder and leading Gershom by the hand.

When the news of their going was brought to Jethro, his face darkened with anger and he sent for two men of the tribe who came swiftly. He said certain words to them and they smiled fiercely and departed. But before they left the encampment they went to a place apart from the other tents and there painted marks on their bodies with red clay, and tied strips of bull-hide round their wrists and ankles; then, with bundles slung from their shoulders, they went away, taking the path that Moses had taken that morning with his wife and sons. But these two went at night and when the sun rose they slept and went on again only when the sun had set.

Moses pitched his tent in a green valley among the foothills. They had travelled some distance in the many days of their journey, and now the edge of the flat land was before them and, beyond the flat land, Egypt. Now he slept, the journey and the task he had undertaken forgotten together; he lay with his head pillowed on his arms and his breath so peaceful it scarcely stirred his beard. On the far side of the tent the boys curled together like puppies exhausted by play. Only Zipporah sat wakeful and watching, her face hollow with weariness and her throat constricted with a fear she could not yet name. She kept a lamp burning but neither the light nor the familiar smoky stench as the wick flared in its shallow saucer of oil, comforted her. She went outside and looked towards the hills they had crossed that day. The moon rode among the stars and the ground was barred with its shadows stretching between the thorn scrub and the acacia trees. 'Lord Sin,' she prayed, addressing the moon by his name, 'give me more light!' And then her eyes caught a glimpse of something that moved, a shadow that slid without sound between the shadows that were still – and yet another. Nothing more. She waited. The shapes were not right. There were the smooth, round shapes of shadows thrown by boulders, the angled pattern of branches, the moon behind them, the sharpness of thorns – but here was a different sharpness, that of no growing thing. These were the shapes of horns . . .

Two men stepped from the shadows into the clear moonlight. They were naked save for anklets and wrist-bands of hide, and their bodies were streaked with red clay. They wore bull-masks, the horns glittering and terrible, and in their hands were knives.

Zipporah moaned and ran inside the tent, her hands plucking at the knots of her girdle where she carried her own knife, a little crescent of sharpened stone. There was no time left for the full rite of the circumcision offering, the dedication and the prayers – time only to do what must be done to save her husband's flesh from the crueller knives of those who had been sent to kill him.

Moses waked from a dark dream into the lamplight, to the stone's touch and the sudden pain, to knowledge of what his wife had done to him. The shock in his eyes turned to loathing as he looked at Zipporah, who flung herself across his knees, weeping. 'Now you are indeed my bridegroom in blood,' she said, through her tears – but he struck her away. The two masked men stood in the tent opening, their heads lowered like the heads of bulls about to charge. Zipporah turned to them and cried, 'See, this man is my bridgroom in blood. Do you dare to use your knives on him who has been given to the god?'

The men shuffled their feet and turned their blades with the points against their own breasts to show that they were, to all intent, unarmed.

'Now go,' said Zipporah, but Moses said, 'Wait,' and, though he spoke quietly, it was with a voice that must be obeyed.

'Shall it be said in later years,' Moses continued, 'that, as I rested on my way to Egypt, Yahweh sought to kill me? And if this is true, how shall it be understood? For I go in Yahweh's name.'

No one answered him.

'Go back to Jethro,' he said, 'and take this woman with you. Tell him that Yahweh's will shall be done as he revealed it to me on the mountain. Tell him also that I shall pass near his tents again – when I bring the people out to worship in the wilderness of Sinai. Let him take back his daughter to dwell in his shadow, and these boys too, for I think they are true children of his tribe. Let him look to their well-being. Go, Zipporah. Had the god required this sacrifice at your hands, surely he would have put it in my mind as a command. And yet you meant no ill; a part of me will grieve at our separation.'

Then he turned his back on them all and they went away, Zipporah in tears and with dragging feet, while Moses set his face towards the border of Egypt.

IO

Word of his coming travelled before him, carried by swift runners from tribe to tribe, yet secretly as though only the dry, sand-laden wind had news of it. When he reached Goshen the people were already waiting, having hurried from their homes and from their work, to see Prince Ra-Mose return.

Aaron was the first to greet him. 'May the Lord Ra-Mose live for ever,' he said, but Moses shook his head and answered, harshly, 'Not Ra-Mose but Moses. I am your brother in blood and your kinsman by marriage, so let there be no more ceremony between us.'

Together they went to Aaron's house, and Aaron spread fresh mats for his guest to lie on, and Elishabeta brought water and poured it over Moses' hands and bathed the dust of his journey from his feet. Later the elders came to give him welcome on behalf of all the Tribes, and with them came Hamor though he had no rightful place in their council.

Aaron said: 'This man is Prince Moses who has returned to us from the wilderness of Sinai, from the mountains beyond the Sea of Reeds. There, between earth and sky, he walked with El, as did Abram in ancient time, and he is charged to lead our people out of Egypt. He is appointed our deliverer.'

The elders murmured together; they had not looked to Egypt for the one the god had promised and their minds were uneasy. Yet Aaron had accepted him. When Hamor spoke, it was for all of them. 'How shall we judge your truth, Prince?' he asked. 'In what name did the god put this task upon you?'

And Moses answered, 'He spoke in the voice of the bull that

84

rides the storm, the overpowering El, and the name by which he charged me is Yahweh, He-who-is.'

Then Hamor asked, 'By what sign shall we know you, servant of Yahweh?'

'By that which I shall do, for Egypt shall spread wide her arms and all the tribes of Israel shall pour out across the plains. Tomorrow I will speak with Pharaoh, and Aaron, whom you trust, shall be my mouth. We will ask for but a respite from your labours, that you may sacrifice and give honour to the god in freedom – but once Egypt is behind us, we will not turn again.'

The elders bowed and retired, satisfied, but Hamor stayed back to say, 'My young warriors are ready. You may call on them.'

Pharaoh was seated, dwarfed by the tall lotus-headed columns that rose on either side of his royal chair. He had no ease in his royalty. The cobra spread her golden hood above his brow, and Nekhebt the vulture, protector of Pharaoh, spanned his breast with her great wings of gold and lapis lazuli. The crook and flail, symbols of power, were in his hands, yet he was nothing; the breath of Osiris had not touched him. Moses, who had walked side by side with the storm while lightning struck the rocks all about him, had more of royalty than Pharaoh had. He smiled and abased himself to the ground.

'Life! Health! Strength!' he said, the god within him speaking to the symbols of the gods that were Pharaoh's.

'These men are ambassadors from the tribes who sit in Goshen,' said the vizier, stooping his shaven head to the king's. 'Does it please Pharaoh to hear their words?'

'Let them speak,' said Pharaoh, and his voice was as cold as water dropping from a stone basin. The vizier turned again to the place where Aaron and Moses waited. His eyes looked through them and he struck the floor with his staff of office.

'Who speaks for the tribes of the Hebrew?' he said. 'Pharaoh hears!'

Moses stood aside to let Aaron speak as was most fitting. Aaron was a priest; the priests of Pharaoh would not set him low.

'The god has put words in my mouth,' said Aaron. 'Thus he says: "The moon approaches the full and the firstlings of our flocks skip in the new grass. Let the people of Israel make a journey of three days into the waste beyond Egypt that they may sacrifice as free men according to the Law." Thus says El, using the mouth of his priest, Aaron.'

Pharaoh sat like a figure of stone, there was no movement to be seen in him – but the flail trembled a little as though he had tensed his hand.

'Who is this god,' he asked, 'that Pharaoh should hear his voice and obey? I do not know your god El, nor do my gods know him.'

Aaron flinched from that cold voice but he answered, 'El has commanded. Let us go, with all our people, for it is death to disobey the mighty one.'

Pharaoh's face was tight with anger and his breast heaved so that the wings of the vulture lifted as though for flight. 'You keep the people from their labours,' he said. 'Go back and tell them that it is also death to disobey Pharaoh. And Pharaoh is the law of *this* land.' A thin smile played at the corners of his mouth. 'Your rebellion stems from idleness,' he added. 'From now on your people shall learn what labour means. Go.'

The audience was at an end.

Those who had waited to hear Pharaoh's reply to Aaron went back to their homes with heavy steps. They hardly knew how to tell their wives the news, for hope had made them young again. And now there was no hope.

Leah was grinding corn in a stone quern, her youngest child kicking his thin legs on a rush mat at her side. When Ishvi came in she looked first at his sorrowing face and then caught the child to her as though she could draw comfort from his innocence.

'The lord El did not speak to Pharaoh,' she said flatly. It was not a question.

'Pharaoh did not hear,' said Ishvi. 'But he saw that the people were idle and, because of that, has put more labours on us.'

'A woman could have told you as much,' said Leah. 'Prince Ra-Mose dreamed a dream in the desert; therefore we must all die. Was there no woman to tell him that the desert is the place of dreams just as it is the place of demons?'

'A man must hope.'

'The hope of our race lies in these little ones,' said Leah, as Zorah had once said, and as she was to say again, and many times. 'Men should listen when their women speak, for *our* knowledge is of the earth.'

Ishvi squatted on the ground beside her and took the child in his arms. 'Leah! Leah!' he chided her. 'Did not the first man heed the first woman – and what good came of it? Let man listen to the god, and let woman listen to her man, for that is the Law.'

'I hear you, husband,' said Leah, dryly, and went again to her work.

Moses went with Aaron into the house where he had been received as an honoured guest. Elishabeta, who had waited with her children about her and such hope in her heart that she could hardly breathe, saw their bowed shoulders, and went

87

away into the inner room that she should not add to their sorrow with her own tears.

Moses said, 'Gather the people together. We must stir their hearts again for they are sick now and ready to die under their burden.'

But Aaron stayed him with a hand on his shoulder. 'Not so. They are hot against you, for what you have done. They had looked for freedom today and have found instead a greater slavery. If you go out to them they will tear you limb from limb.'

'Yet I will go out to them,' said Moses. 'And I will make them hear.'

But they would not listen. It was *they* who determined to make *him* hear and his voice was lost beneath their voices. Some threw stones and Aaron had to drag the prince back into the house while the stones still thudded against the door. Moses writhed on the ground and beat upon it with his fists, raging against Yahweh who had sent him on this thankless mission and then betrayed him before Pharaoh.

'We will go to Pharaoh again,' said Aaron. 'Together we will make this little painted king feel the weight of your god, even over the whole land of Egypt. He will hear you, Moses.'

The next morning they went early to the river and waited for Pharaoh to come out for his day's sport. A cool breeze ruffled the water, lifting the light papyrus rafts so that they nudged and jostled each other at the bank. Now Pharaoh might be seen without the trappings of his exalted state – a man dressed in white linen, a wide gold collar at his throat, his fishing spears in his hand. Any one of the nobles with him would have made as fine a king, but only he was escorted by slaves bearing fans of ostrich plumes.

Moses, with Aaron beside him, stood in Pharaoh's path and

this time Moses did not abase himself, for as men they were equal. Without taking his eyes from Pharaoh's eyes, he bade Aaron stretch out his staff above the water.

'Now,' he said, 'let Pharaoh see the power of Israel's god. Look how the water has been turned to blood and how the fish die in it, floating with their bellies upward. Look long, Pharaoh, and when the people of Egypt cry out for water, when their cattle die and their children die, remember that the god of Israel has done this thing because you would not let his people go.'

Pharaoh looked. It was as Moses said. The river flowed red and, as far as his eyes could see, dead carcasses of fish drifted to the surface, their white underbellies catching the sun's light.

'Here's sport for Pharaoh,' said Moses softly. 'And it will be the same tomorrow and the next day and the next until you let the Tribes go free to make their sacrifice in the wilderness beyond your borders.'

Pharaoh recoiled from the sight. Already he heard the wailing of his people as their crops and their livestock died, and he put his hands over his ears so that he should not hear. But his companion, Bes-En-Seset, whose name meant Flame of Fire, ran to the priests and magicians in the city and brought them back with him to the river bank. They laughed when they saw the fear in Pharaoh's eyes.

'Look again, Pharaoh,' they said, and he looked and the water was clear, the fish darting between strands of weed. 'And again,' said the magicians, and they stretched out their wands above the water as Aaron had done, changing it to blood again, even as Pharaoh watched.

'It is simple magic,' said the chief of the magicians. 'Any man can do this if he so wills. The high god of Israel must learn a greater magic than he has shown here if he wishes to bend Pharaoh to his command.'

For seven more days Moses sat in Aaron's house and the god still slept though he sought him with prayer and fasting.

'You have commanded me, Lord Yahweh,' he cried. 'You have marked me with your seal and taken me from the tents of Midian to serve your purpose. I have redeemed my life from your hands with my blood, as the lives of my sons have been redeemed, with theirs. I have become one with your people, so that I breathe with their breath. I have taken Abram for my father and I claim that which you promised him between the divided sacrifice in the hills of Canaan. In Abram's name I claim it, and in my own, for so you promised me on your holy mountain . . .'

Outside in the fields and brickyards of Egypt, the women of Israel slaved that their husbands might find a little ease at noon, a little longer respite at night. The flat clay bricks were strengthened with straw to prevent their crumbling too soon in the sun's heat, and always the straw had been provided. Now, because Moses and Aaron had stood tall before Pharaoh, the labourers must find their own straw, yet each day's tally of finished bricks must be the same. So the women and children spread and dried the long stalks, tied them in bales and carried them on their backs to where their menfolk moulded the clay. Old grandmothers who had thought to end their days in rest, now tended the fires and baked bread again, jigging the babies on their knees while the babies cried for their mothers who were too busy to heed them.

And Moses brandished his fists at the empty sky and groaned aloud.

'Peace, brother,' said Aaron. 'The moon moves to the appointed place. Let us make our sacrifice here in Goshen and perhaps the god will speak again . . .'

'We will sacrifice in the wilderness,' said Moses, between his teeth. 'And until we have left the dust of Egypt behind us I will neither sleep nor eat. I will be a thorn in Pharaoh's side to goad him; I will be a scorpion beneath the sole of his foot!'

Visions of plague and pestilence rose before his eyes and haunted him. The croaking of frogs in the marshes multiplied and filled his mind so that it seemed to him that he had only to speak the word and all the frogs in Egypt would come to his bidding, swarming across the ground and into the houses, even into the ovens and kneading bowls so that the very bread on the Egyptians' tables was compounded of frogs, all alive and croaking. But his exaltation was not long, for there came the priests and magicians of Pharaoh, never hurrying, and they laughed and the frogs were nothing. 'We also can conjure frogs out of the air,' they said. 'This Yahweh is but a little god.'

A gnat skimmed about his head and stung his lip. He put up his hand to brush it away and saw his hand black against the sky, and below it the gnats swarmed, settling where they would on man and beast, a torment to every living creature. But Pharaoh's magicians came, slowly and smiling, and they too could create gnats from the dust of the earth. It no longer mattered that Pharaoh was but a man – his word could command where the word of the god was not heard at all.

'May the plague fall on him!' cried Moses, spittle flying from his lips. 'May the plague eat Egypt, the cattle and the flocks and the people too!' And he saw the plague creep over the land in the likeness of a mottled arm and, wherever it touched, the people and the cattle died. And now the magicians stood silent, for this was not the work of a little god.

In the inner room, Elishabeta sat with Aaron and the children. She heard Moses call out in a high, inhuman voice, and she clung fearfully to her husband. The smallest of the children ran to his elder brother and hid his face.

'What does he do?' whispered Elishabeta. 'Oh, my husband, why did you take this man to be your brother?'

'Hush!' Aaron answered her. 'He seeks to rouse the god.'

Even as he spoke a storm burst overhead. Lightning cracked the sky and the ground quaked. Rain drummed on the roofs and on the tents with a sound like the beating of many staves. Moses stood in the door-place and peered into the tumultuous dark, his eyes hot and red from wakefulness. The high vault of heaven was on fire and among the flames the bull rushed, massive shoulders gleaming with sweat, head down and nostrils smoking. The bull was awake. He had come from Midian to lead the people out.

Moses ran from house to house, calling the people to come out for the rider of the storm was abroad. There was an urgency in his voice that brought them hurrying to believe – though they had stoned him but seven days before. Now they stood in groups and gazed at the sky, and some saw the bull, glorious in anger, snorting and pounding the thunderclouds with his hooves. Others saw nothing but rain and the storm-devils dancing in the red dust. But all agreed that a fire was kindled in Moses, a spark fanned to life by the god's breath – they would follow him now wherever he led, though it were to the gates of Sheol, the haunt of demons. They would sacrifice in whatever place he chose.

Ishvi ordered Leah to put together their household things, the rugs and pots and the little clay images of the gods.

'The Lord Moses has gone again to Pharaoh,' he said, 'and the elders of the Tribes are with him.'

'What is that to us?' said Leah. 'Twice before have they stood before Pharaoh's majesty – and the god of Moses did not speak then. Shall he speak now because there is thunder in the air? Rather should you sleep, my husband, for tomorrow is another day of heaviness, and *that* was laid on you by Lord Moses' hand.'

'Tomorrow is the first day of another life,' said Ishvi, 'but even if that were not so, this was already ordained a night of watching. Had you forgotten it is the feast of first fruits? The moon sails in her full strength and the lambs have been led to the slaughter.'

Leah sprang to her feet, all contrition. 'Indeed I had forgotten. The storm drove it from my head together with every other thought save for that of the children. The smallest one is truly a blessing, he wakes only to feed and sleeps again, but Naboth and Zillah have fretted all day with the prickling heat. Now they also sleep. Ishvi, have a care for Naboth. Do not make him a man too soon.'

'He will grow to manhood in the sweet hills of Canaan,' said Ishvi, his eyes shining. 'And Naaman too. They will walk as proud as Abram, and El-Shaddai will walk with them ...'

Leah silenced him with her work-roughened hand upon his mouth.

'And they will be plagued by devils too, like your Lord Moses, I don't doubt. Ah, we women must protect you all in the end. We listen to your dreams, and bear your children, and sprinkle blood at our doors to keep the demons away from your sleeping. We are at the beginning and ending of all your lives from the moment we lift you naked from between the birth-stones to the hour when we pinch your eyes closed in your last sleep. Where would you men be if there were no women to work for you and wail for you? Yet you think nothing of it; you must be for ever looking to the gods for comfort.'

Like her mother, she had a quick, scolding tongue but she went willingly to gather up the household things, setting the little ones among the bundles so gently that they did not waken. When the lamb was brought in she made her face solemn and, taking a bunch of hyssop, sprinkled the door-post with its blood as the custom had been since the beginning of time. Then, on her knees, she served the meat to her husband as her mother had served her father until the year he died.

As they ate, men came to warn them to keep their homes that night and not to venture out whatever sound they heard. These were young men, their faces dabbled with blood and wearing rams' horns curling about their ears. Their eyes were gleaming and dangerous and they carried sharp knives unsheathed. Some had even slashed the skin of their bare breasts and forearms to show the gods that they were men of blood, fearing no hurt. When they left each dwelling the lamps were extinguished, one by one, until every house and every tent lay dark and quiet under the sky. The thunder had died away.

Then from the wilderness beyond the city came a drumming, faint and rapid, the separate beats running together to make a sound like the first lifting of the wind before a desert-storm, when the sand dances above the rocks in spirals no higher than a man's knee. Louder it grew until it was like the beating of great wings overhead, and still louder. Those who listened might have heard too the sound of running feet, but they stopped their ears. The women veiled their eyes and stooped over their children, hiding them in the folds of their garments.

'Hush!' breathed Ishvi, as much to comfort himself as Leah. 'These are surely the winged messengers of El; they have come to smite the Egyptians as Prince Moses said. Our houses they will spare because of the sprinkled blood. But do not listen, Leah, my dove!'

After that there was silence until the moon went down and the sun showed his first light in the east. Ishvi raised his wife and took her out into the waking morning. All that they possessed they hung in panniers across the back of the cow; the small girl, Zillah, straddled the calf and her father's arm was ready to support her. Leah carried the fire-stones and kindling in a leather-pouch at her girdle, and Naaman, the baby, hung at her back in a sling of soft wool. Naboth, the elder boy, with eight summers to strengthen his legs, walked behind with the goats – five goats, a great responsibility!

Already the ways were thronged with people, themselves laden or leading pack-animals, or driving their beasts before them. And many laughed and sang as they went, for the Egyptians, in their new haste to see the Hebrew go, had pressed gifts upon them, gold and bronze, carnelian and lapis lazuli, and clothing too, and asses weighed down with household stuff; also flocks and herds they gave to them, so that not even the thought of the wilderness ahead could quench their spirits.

The Egyptians watched them go. The men stood with faces like stone, their hands heavy at their sides. They were like a grove of stone figures or like the carved *ushabtis* that accompany the dead into the darkness of the tomb. Behind the walls and in the courtyards women wept for their first-born sons, each one slain between dusk and dawn, and in the pastures behind the houses, neglected cows, their udders heavy with milk, lowed their need to a world too bereft to care.

Thus, while the gods of Egypt slept, the god of Israel led his people out, with all that they possessed, to begin their long journey to the land he had promised Abram.

I I

That evening they camped at Succoth, a place of leafy groves and sweet water. Fires were lit and the women brought out the dough they had prepared in Egypt, and baked flat cakes in the embers.

'It grieves me to offer you such strange bread as this, my husband,' said Leah. 'There was no time to leaven it and let it rise. But eat, Ishvi, and rest; the day has been long.'

As they lay at ease, Moses went from fire to fire, to every family, and spoke with them. He took the bread in his hands and broke it, saying to each one, 'This is the bread of deliverance. Let every generation eat it and, eating, remember that this day you were brought out of bondage by the hand of Yahweh.'

This was the first time Leah had seen the Prince since the night he had left their house with Hamor seeking him, so long ago, and she marvelled at the change in him – a change that went deeper than the thinness of his bearded face, and the timbre of his voice. She looked into his black, fanatical eyes and shivered. But Ishvi called Naboth to him and said, 'Did you hear? This is the bread of deliverance. Eat.' The boy crumbled the bread in his hand and, tasting it, said, 'It is not so very different from other bread.' Ishvi laughed and answered, 'But that was the bread of bitterness, eaten with bitter herbs – chicory and pepperwort and snake-root. It is very different.'

Leah smiled to see them so happy but in her mind she already looked back to Egypt where Zorah and Rebekkah, her parents, were buried together. 'It is not good to separate the old from the young, the dead from the living,' she thought.

'We have left behind us the bones of our ancestors – where will our own bones lie?'

Ishvi saw her smile fade and guessed her thoughts. 'Do not look back, my dear one,' he said. 'Remember the lesson of Lot's wife, and look only forward.'

'Tell me about Lot's wife,' Zillah clamoured, and wriggled close to her father. 'Tell me!'

Ishvi hugged her. 'It was long ago in the ancient times,' he said, beginning the familiar tale, 'when our first-father Abram pitched his tents in the high country while his brother Lot went down into the plains, to the very gates of the city . . .'

'That was a great place,' Zillah interrupted, for she knew the story well. 'A great place with houses and markets and people – '

'And wickedness! Such wickedness that Almighty El was resolved to destroy it, together with Gomorrah, its twin city.'

Zillah shuddered, pleasurably.

'But Abram, that upright man – '

'Like Grandfather Zorah?'

'Like Grandfather Zorah.' Ishvi sighed. 'Zillah, do you wish to hear this story? Then be quiet and still. Abram dared to argue with the Great Spirit and bargained with him for the lives of the people. "If you can find me fifty righteous men in the cities, then – for their sakes – will I hold back the storm," said El.

'But not fifty were found, nor even forty. Nor thirty. So Abram went again to the place where the god walked, and pleaded for the lives of twenty law-respecting men, or even ten. Yet though he searched through all the teeming alleys of the cities from dawn to starlight, he could not find the ten he sought. And El would bargain no more – except for this. If Abram, he said, so wished, he might warn his brother Lot with his wife and family so that they could leave the city in safety before he loosed his wrath. Our father Abram prostrated himself before the god and rose and went again to the city though this time the way was fearful; the ground shivered and rocked beneath his feet and great cracks appeared in the walls of the houses. He found his brother Lot with his wife and daughters huddled together, and he led them by safe paths until they were clear of the place, and he begged them, "*Do not look back!*"

'But Lot's wife, a true daughter of the mother whose devouring curiosity brought about the fall of mankind, looked back – and behold! where she had stood, a breathing woman with bracelets on her arms, and her bare feet light on the grass, there was nothing more than a tall pillar of salt that the cattle would lick until it was all worn away.

'Then El let loose the storm and the two cities were destroyed so completely that no stone was left standing upon another, and only a stink and a great smoke remained . . .'

Ishvi looked across the fire to Leah. 'As Abram led his brother safe from the anger of El-Shaddai, so does Prince Moses lead us from beneath Pharaoh's shadow. And Abram was also a stranger in the land, even as Moses is. Trust him, Leah.'

The great trade-route from Egypt to the land of the Philistines led from the city of the moon-god, Sin, and went direct to Gaza, a journey of no hardship. But Moses and Aaron had brought the people southwards to Succoth, and now turned north once more, halting at Etham on the edge of the wilderness.

'It is in his mind to take the other road,' said old Kedemah, knowledgeably. 'We will cross the Wilderness of Shur, by the way that passes through Beer-Sheba and up into the hills of Hebron, where Abram once built an altar . . .'

But it was soon apparent that this was not to be. North they went again, towards the city of Pi-ha-hiroth and here Moses hesitated and turned back a little to camp between the city and the Sea of Reeds.

'He follows the cloud,' said Kedemah, pointing. 'For has he not said that Yahweh speaks to him from the storm?' Though he spoke with confidence, his mind was troubled. Time was passing and this was surely not the road to freedom.

Aaron drew Moses aside and asked him to reveal at least some part of his plan. 'The people are growing afraid,' he said, 'and with cause, I think. Unless we make more haste, Pharaoh will rouse himself and follow us.'

Prince Moses sniffed the air and looked towards the sea. 'Patience,' he answered. 'If Pharaoh follows, as he surely will, he shall have yet another proof that Yahweh is mightier than all men. But now is the time of waiting. Tell the people, if you will, that they shall not wait long.' Then he called Hamor to him and bade him see that the people were ready to move when he should give the command.

'We are hemmed in by the wilderness,' said Micael, saying only what many thought. 'It is not easy to quit Egypt after all. We have passed two border townships without hindrance because Pharaoh knows that we can go no further. We have no wings to bear us across the waste of water; he can stretch out his arm and take us when he wills.'

'The Prince has appointed watchers,' said Ephraim, his neighbour. 'They look constantly towards Egypt, therefore he expects pursuit once the Egyptians have finished their time of mourning . . .'

Even as he spoke there came a sound of shouting from the outskirts of the camp, and in a moment everyone was afoot and hurrying towards the waterside. Pharaoh's time of mourning had been short indeed.

'They call this the Sea of Reeds,' Kedemah said, bitterly, 'yet after this night it may well be called the Sea of Tears. Pharaoh's army is so close behind us that I smell the sweat of its horses and hear the rumble of the chariot wheels . . .'

It was not far from the truth. The Egyptians were as yet but a haze of dust in the distance but their approach was rapid and the sea stretched before, impassable. The people of Israel went here and there along the bank, searching for a fording-place, but in the evening light they could not tell the shallows from the deeps; there was a constant shiver across the surface of the water and the papyrus reeds, from which the sea took its name, bent and whispered.

Above the opposite shore the strange, smoking cloud they had observed all day hung in the air, a blood-hued nimbus surrounding it. The first stars appeared. The dusk-darkened reeds swayed in a sudden fierce wind from the east, and slowly the water ebbed away. 'Now!' cried Moses and he began to run, with long, leaping strides, across the puddled space. Aaron followed with his wife and children and the pack-beasts. And then suddenly all the people were crowding together in haste to get to the other side – a throng of pushing bodies, hurrying feet, beasts plunging and bellowing as their drivers goaded them on, laden asses stepping delicately, tossing anxious heads.

In the press, Leah lost her hold on Ishvi's arm and was swept away from him, her wail lost in the shouts and curses that rose all round her. Hooves churned up the mud, children screamed. Those who had safely made their passage held flaming torches to light the path for others and the red glare illuminated what seemed to be a vision of Sheol where the spirits of departed men struggled and stretched out their hands for life.

'How long will El's hand hold back the waters?' thought Leah. 'Will it be long enough to let so large a multitude across?' She prayed that the children were safe, and Ishvi with his broad back and gentle heart, and the precious cow and the calf, and the goats. They were so wayward, the goats – surely they would break free and go back again!

But at length it was over; the last old man, mud-splashed

and panting, hauled up the further bank, the last of the flocks whacked and clouted into safety. And it was not too soon. Already the first of the pursuing Egyptians crushed the reeds beneath their chariot-wheels, the torch-flare lighting the bronze of harness and body armour. A shower of spears arched across the space and fell short. The horses strained and sweated, and the wheels, clogged with mud, refused to turn. The warriors leapt from their chariots and came on, while Moses watched their advance, his eyes expressionless. With these same men, perhaps, he had marched and fought, shared meat and drink with them, planned campaigns – but that had been long ago, in a different life.

The wind dropped and the water, no longer held back by its strong blowing, turned again. The Egyptians were caught, their chariots sinking deeper in the slime, impossible to shift. The horses reared, their hooves striking at those who sought to free them from their harness; the flower of Pharaoh's armies was lost under the waves. Some struggled home, broken wretches, to describe an event they could not have changed.

'Men we can fight,' they said, 'but we did not go against men. Can a sea be fought with spears and arrows? That people has a leader whose magic is stronger than weapons. It is well to see them go.'

Sobbing, Leah searched for Ishvi among the crowds. Pity for the Egyptians squeezed at her heart, she felt even the tips of her fingers heavy with sorrow for the wives and mothers of all those drowned men, and for Pharaoh too, who was – beneath the weight of his double crown – only a boy. What if her own Naboth's hands had been made to wield a crook and flail instead of a stick to prod goats? What if Ishvi had been a warrior?

And where was Ishvi now? Where were the children? All had come safely across the Sea of Reeds, that she knew. She need not fear for their lives – but where and how could she find them? Those about her were strangers, not even sons of the Tribes but others who had thrown in their lot with Israel, to escape or die; they could not help her to find her husband. Her head ached from the babble of tongues, her body was bruised from the jostling, the cries and prayers of the Egyptians still rang in her ears. Yet here were people laughing! They reacted to freedom as men with weak heads do to strong drink. They reached out their hands to catch at passing women and embraced them, kissing them, and the women looked so bold, not minding though their own husbands stood near by. Leah felt shame for them and, holding her muddied skirts close to her, edged away, avoiding the noisiest groups and hardly caring which way she went – one way was as good as another since Ishvi might be anywhere.

There was a sound of wild music and she walked towards it. In spite of her anxiety her heart warmed to the beat, the drums and cymbals and the high, reedy note of the pipe. It was a dance of triumph, stirring the blood, raising the flagging spirits; under its spell Leah remembered that the Egyptians had been the enemy, the oppressors, and the tears dried on her cheeks.

In a space cleared for her at the water's edge, Miriam danced. Her face was streaked with white and her hair, dressed in a thousand tiny plaits, each tipped with gold, swung about her shoulders. She looked noble and free as the first Eve must have looked, and she was decked from head to foot in the spoils of Egypt. Gold circled her arms and ankles, gold chains hung from her waist, and on her breast a great gold pectoral ornament displayed its pattern of lions and lotuses, and all this gold made music as she stamped and whirled, beating upon a *tabret*, a small hand-drum, and chanting:

'Give praise to Yahweh for he has triumphed,

See where the horse and his rider he has hurled
    beneath the waves,
Pharaoh's chariots he has cast into the sea.
Who is like Yahweh among all the gods?
We come, the Chosen of Yahweh,
The ground trembles at our passing.
The chiefs of Edom shall be dismayed,
The chiefs of Moab shall be dismayed,
Through the whole land of Canaan the people
    shall be dismayed.
Who is like Yahweh, among all the gods?
We come, the redeemed of Yahweh,
He will set us upon his mountain,
Upon his holy mountain, where is his sanctuary.
We will praise him upon his mountain.
Who is like Yahweh, among all the gods?'

Other women joined her, stamping the rhythm on the earth
with their bare feet, and Leah too might have gone with them,
husband and family forgotten, had not a hand at her elbow
recalled her to herself.

It was Kedemah, her father-in-law, who had come in search
of her, leaving his son to watch over the family and keep them
together. He looked old and meagre and undignified, his
clothes torn and a bruise darkening beneath one eye. He looked
at Miriam with savage disapproval and said: 'I had not expected
to find my son's wife cavorting like a she-demon among
strangers,' but his voice trembled with relief. 'Come you to
your children. My little Naaman cries for his mother.'

And Leah was too glad to see him to mind the injustice of
his accusation. Supporting each other, they moved away and
the chanting faded behind them.

12

That day they rested and the following night and then they went on. For three whole days they saw no water at all; their speed slackened and they looked back constantly. On the fourth day those in front cried, 'Water!' and began to run. They all ran, stumbling and shouting with gladness. But the water, when they reached it, was brackish and undrinkable. The people drank and spat; even the beasts backed away, shaking their heads and snorting. The women sank to the ground, turning reproachful eyes on their menfolk. They must drink or die.

'It is not bad water,' said Moses. 'See how the ground is green all around. These trees take moisture from the earth with their thirsty roots, and flourish ...'

'People are not trees,' said Hamor. 'It can do them no good if every drop they take in their mouths to swallow, they must vomit forth again. If you cannot give them water their bellies will accept, they will kill you.'

'Then Yahweh must sweeten the water,' said Moses,' and he smiled. Hobab, Jethro's shepherd son, had taught him many skills, among them the art of purifying unpalatable streams with the leaves of a certain tree ... and that tree grew nearby.

'Fill your vessels and waterskins,' he ordered. 'Surely the god who brought you safely across the Sea of Reeds has not forgotten you. Fill every carrier you possess and bring them all to me.'

They doubted his power but obeyed. Still smiling, he cut branches from the tree and scattered the leaves in the water. 'In a little while,' he told them, 'you will drink your fill.'

And it was true. They drank and filled their waterskins again, and went on with springing steps.

'They are children,' said Moses. 'They look for signs and wonders. But we must make men of them before we can hope to conquer the land across the Jordan.'

Then they left that place and went on to Elim where there were twelve springs, bubbling clear and pure, and many palm trees. There Moses let them stay a while to refresh their spirits, for he knew that the next stage of their journey would try them hard. Now they must cross the Wilderness of Sin, the ancient moon-god – a place of drought and terrible, burning heat in which no living thing could thrive. Yet cross it they must to reach the sacred mountain, Horeb, to renew the covenant as he planned to do.

The level in the waterskins sank lower; the bags hung slack and flaccid across the backs of the animals. Each evening brought the bitter choice – whether to let the children or the beasts first quench their thirsts. 'Without our beasts, we die,' said one, but another answered, 'Without our children it were as though we had never been born.' And the little ones stood about, dull-eyed and weary.

Ahead the dry land shimmered; sometimes the ghost of a green *wadi* might be seen, inverted, in the sky, giving the people hope for a little while. But the hope died.

Kedemah shrivelled a little more each day. Surreptitiously he shared his own allowance of water with the baby, Naaman, courting his own death with a gallantry he had never shown in his life. Sores broke out on his lips and his teeth loosened in his head but such matters no longer worried him. He grumbled merely from old habit.

'It was madness to come this way,' he said. 'There is a direct route between Egypt and Canaan – one that the traders use.

We might have made sacrifice to Prince Moses' god in the land of the promise, had he listened to the elders from the beginning.'

'But that was not the command,' said Ishvi. 'We must trust him entirely or we are all lost . . .' His voice failed as he looked at the children, and at Leah, who slept with Naaman held to her dry breast. The baby whimpered, too weak to cry, and Kedemah put out his thin hand to stroke the thin cheek.

Ishvi poured a little of the precious water into a flat dish and moistened a piece of rag which he gave to Naaman to suck. He took Zillah on his knees and touched her lips with water, and then Naboth's. The rest he set down for the cow, saying, 'Drink, sister, and make milk for us.' The cow turned her soft and sorrowing gaze to his and drank.

'We must trust Prince Moses,' Ishvi said again to Kedemah. 'Remember Marah, the water of bitterness that he made sweet for us with green branches. He will bring us to water again.'

'There are water-holes in plenty between Egypt and Canaan,' insisted Kedemah. 'And those are sweet enough without any intervention from either man or god. If we trust Prince Moses too far he will kill us all.' But he cared only for Naaman's sake.

'He will kill us all,' Zillah echoed.

And so it seemed, for the desert rolled endlessly before them, parched earth and rock; withered shrubs, brittle and bone-white; dried gullies where streams had once raced. Now a demon walked with them in a rustle of invisible wings, touching one here and another there – and those he touched, died – first the very old and the very young, then others who should have been in the prime of their lives. There was no time for proper mourning beyond the raising of little heaps of stones to cover the indignity of death. The survivors reeled on and their wailing was like a canopy above their heads on which the sun beat without mercy.

Micael's wife, Sarai, was one of the first to fall. Her steps grew slower and slower till, with a little cry, she dropped to her knees. Smiling so that her children should not be afraid, she struggled to her feet, stumbled a little further and fell again. There was amazement in her eyes. Then she coughed and it was over. Micael tried to lift her but even so slight a weight as hers was too great for his diminished strength to bear. Ishvi helped him to gather stones to keep her small corpse safe from the jackals' feasting. When that was done Micael brandished his fists at the sky and cursed the day of the exodus from Egypt.

'If I ever trust an Egyptian again,' he shouted, 'may *Aluqah*, the flesh-eater, devour me – may the *Ziyyim* of the desert tear my bones apart . . .'

Leah went to him and put her hand on his forehead, drawing her fingers down, closing his eyes, his mouth. 'Micael, Micael! Even the emptiness of earth and sky has ears. Bring the little ones to us. We will share all that we have and, when that is gone, we will share our hunger, Micael, as you and Ishvi once shared your labours in Goshen . . .'

Micael groaned but the violence had left him at Leah's touch. 'She was so small,' he said, 'like the little birds that hide among the corn-stalks and fly up, singing and chattering, when the scythes move behind them. She never complained. When the ass died and she was forced to walk, her tears were for the unlucky beast, not one for herself. The children dragged at her skirts and she took their hands and told stories so that they forgot their parched mouths and empty bellies. If any of us deserved to lie down in the green land of Canaan, she did. Yet she is dead.'

'We must all die,' said Leah. 'How many of us will do so

with a smile on our lips and kindness in our hearts? You were greatly blessed in Sarai, your wife. Bring your children to us.'

Many looked back to the old life in Egypt with longing as though it were a garden they had left behind, a place of tree-shaded pools where plump fish rose to be taken in the hand, where every meal was a feast and every evening melodious with the sound of flute and tabor.

'It was not like that,' Ishvi told them, squatting with the men in the red dust. But even those who remembered the lean days of Israel's bondage turned on him with bitter tongues.

'It was not good,' they said, 'yet it was a settled place. It was not walking between death and death, stalked by jackals and circled by kites and vultures. The desert is littered with our bones – and there was ease of a sort in Egypt.'

'It is the same for us all,' said Ishvi wearily. He might have added, 'For Prince Moses too.' That was in his heart to say, but these others would not have accepted it. Perhaps they thought their leader sat apart in a rich tent, waited on by servants, feasting where they starved, but Ishvi knew better. He had seen Prince Moses weep for Micael's wife, and noticed how he had put out his tongue to lick away the salt tears. There was hunger in that face, as much as in any man's.

So they continued from day to day, from water-hole to water-hole where there was often only mud to soothe their cracked lips. The pace was so slow that not even the weakest could fail to keep up with the rest. Now, reluctantly, they began to slaughter their beasts, taking first those that were older or more lame. The meat was tough and flavourless but it kept life in them.

Ishvi took the white cow by her horns and put the edge of his knife to her throat, turning his face away from the reproach in her eyes. Her hide was dark with sweat and dust and she trembled constantly as though fear ran under her skin. Ishvi, with the knife in his hand, spoke gentle words to her, remembering that she had been a calf of the cow Leah had brought him as her marriage-piece, a white cow, unblemished.

'It is for the little ones,' he told her, 'for Naboth and Naaman and Zillah, and for Micael's children . . .'

Once again he raised the knife and again hesitated, for there came the sound of hurrying feet and Micael was beside him, panting from his haste.

'Do not be so quick, brother,' he said. 'This creature of yours will be needed in the land of Canaan. If we kill the cows how shall new herds be made?'

'You are mad,' said Ishvi. 'How shall we even reach Canaan unless we eat?'

'Food drops from the sky; we have only to gather it. Come and see, Ishvi, if you do not believe me. Come.'

He half-dragged, half-carried his brother through the camp to where the whole people gathered, far fewer than had left Egypt, and a great hush was upon them all. Across the wilderness, flying low, their wings heavy with weariness, came flocks of quail and more and more until the ground was thick with them.

That night, when they had eaten, Ishvi said, 'Now tell me, Micael, whence came these birds?' and Micael, wiping the grease from his lips, shrugged and answered, 'Who knows?'

'And who cares?' thought Leah, watching the children, sprawled asleep. Naboth, as though he felt his mother's eyes upon him, turned and belched, without waking. 'Who cares?' she asked aloud. 'It was good food. We have given thanks for it.' She nodded towards the small clay figures of the gods, whose feet she had smeared with blood. But Ishvi still looked to Micael for a reply. 'Who knows? Who cares? That is no answer. I say that we were hungry and have been fed. Did not Prince Moses have a hand in this?'

Leah flung up her hands and cried, 'Prince Moses! Prince Moses! If we must thank him because we have eaten, where then shall we lay the blame for our hunger?'

'What happened, Micael?' he asked again.

Micael said, slowly, 'Yes, there was surely magic in it. Some of us had gone together in a group to speak with the Prince. We were from all the Tribes but a son of Reuben was our spokesman. I do not know what was in our minds to say, but despair sat on our shoulders. Perhaps we wanted to turn about for Egypt – to offer hostages and make our peace with Pharaoh – I cannot say. Perhaps we only wished to state our case, to display our hunger and our rags.' He scratched his head in perplexity. 'We have grumbled enough to each other; today we took our complaints to the leaders.'

'And then?'

'Hamor guarded the opening of Prince Moses' tent. Our brother Hamor. He had a tall spear in his hand and he turned it against us, against me. But Prince Moses came out and bade him put his spear aside and he came seven paces to meet us. Aaron, the son of Amram, was with him, and Miriam the priestess, one on either side. The Prince bowed his head and listened. When we had finished he stared out across the desert, quite silent, as though he listened to some other voice. Then he smiled. What voice spoke in his head I know not, but he smiled. He raised his staff and pointed towards the horizon, the thin edge between land and sky. We looked and there was a cloud. It drew nearer, Ishvi, and it was not a cloud but the birds. Then Prince Moses cried out, "Yahweh has heard your lamentations; he has compassion for your hunger. Eat, my children." The rest you know.'

'Ah well,' said Leah, charitably. 'We have been fed and that is enough for our minds to deal with at one time. And our good cow is spared.' If only old Kedemah had lived to see this day . . . ah! perhaps it was *he* who had sent the quails – such power the dead wielded. She would say nothing to Ishvi, but from the next meal she would set aside the choicest portion as an offering to her father-in-law's friendly ghost that he would not wander, hungry, in Sheol.

There were no more quails but, with their bellies full again, the Tribes went forward without grumbling and before long reached the foothills of Mount Horeb where there was pasture. Now they moved through groves of tamarisks and the land fed them from its sweetness. Each morning the ground beneath the low, shrubby trees was white with a strange dew that dissolved with the rising of the sun.

'This you may eat,' said Moses, 'but let no man gather more than he needs for himself and his family for it does not keep from one day even to the next. Be sure there will be another harvest tomorrow.'

Ishvi went before Leah and tasted it. The doubt left his eyes at once. 'It is sweet,' he said. 'It is like wafers made with honey. How right we were to put our trust in this man . . .'

Leah smiled, herself all sweetness, and said, 'It is in Ishvi, my husband, that I put my trust. Have I not told you so before? And what has Prince Moses to do with this? The honey-bread that lies upon the ground is from the earth and therefore the gift of the Mother. You should not neglect to thank *her*, Ishvi.'

Ishvi held her close. 'Is it not dew?' he asked, teasing her. 'It falls from the sky, Leah, my wife, and is the gift of the Father. Do not neglect to thank *him*!'

Now the Tribes camped on Horeb itself, where swathes of green clothed the rock. Here they must wait until Prince Moses had ratified again the covenant between his god and the people. It was a time of renewal and replacement; a time for the mending of tents and garments, of making new pots and platters; a time for sorting and marking the beasts that had survived the journey, of counting and setting aside the losses each family had sustained, of making new alliances and betrothals. Many disputes were brought to Moses for judgement, so many that he sat from dawn to sunset advising and ordering until his wits were dulled by fatigue and, when he rose at night to go within his tent, he walked like an old man.

The people talked no more of returning to Egypt. The honey-tasting dew-fall of each day sweetened their tempers as it strengthened their bodies; they laughed as they worked, and set no guards about the camp for they were ready to welcome the whole world if the world should come in peace. There was no argument, they believed, too deep for Prince Moses to settle, no tangle of inheritance too complicated for him to unravel – as he decided such matters between brother and brother and dealt fairly between them, so would he deal fairly between his people and any strangers who might come.

While they rested here, Jethro came with many of his tribesmen and pitched his black tents a little way down the valley. The Israelites left their tasks and went to greet these distant kinsmen, eager for the exchange of news. But Prince Moses did not go.

'He is too proud,' said Zipporah. 'He sent me away from him. He will not come to you lest it appear he looks for my return.'

'Then I will go to him,' said Jethro, 'for my own pride is of a different sort.'

Moses was sitting before his tent, ringed about with people, when Jethro came, bringing Zipporah with him, and the boys. The people made a pathway for them but stayed as close as they were able for their were curious to see the woman who, rumour said, was their Prince's wife, but they saw little, since she was heavily veiled.

'Neither tall nor low in stature,' Leah told Zillah in later years, 'and so wrapped about in cloth that only her eyes showed and they were huge and mournful, black-shadowed like the eyes of an Egyptian woman. Above her brow hung many discs of gold, bright in the noonday sun, and she had bracelets on her arms and rings about her ankles, and little bells of bronze and silver that made a sort of music as she walked. Yes, and the palms of her hands were stained red with henna. But Prince Moses would not look at her.'

Those who stood nearest him said that, when he saw his father-in-law, Prince Moses' face set in rigid lines; he looked like a man marked out by death and the breath heaved in his chest. But he greeted the old man with proper courtesy, embracing him, and the children he took by their hands and looked at them for a long time.

Jethro said, 'I know now that Yahweh called you away from Midian that his purpose should be fulfilled. I did not know it then and you went without my blessing. That blessing I bring you, Moses.'

Moses answered him in a level voice, 'On my road from Midian two men followed me. That much you know. Yet I accept your blessing, Jethro, and what happened I do not hold against you.'

'I have brought, also, Zipporah, your wife,' said Jethro, 'and your sons that they may grow to manhood in their father's tent.'

'We will talk,' said Moses, and he led his father-in-law away to a place where their speech would be more private.

While they talked, the sun moved across the heavens and was already on his downward path before they had finished.

During all this time Zipporah stood erect and still, looking straight before her, Gershom at her side. No word passed between them and when food was brought they would not eat. The little boy, Eliazar, stood for as long as he could but he looked anxiously and often at his mother's face. At last he could stand no longer and sat down, cross-legged, at her feet. He did not refuse the food but, when he had eaten a little, his brother lightly touched his shoulder, and he put the rest aside.

When Jethro came from Moses' tent he did not speak but Zipporah asked a question with her eyes, reading the answer in his. She turned and followed him from the camp and the boys walked behind them. Moses watched them go.

13

From that day the Prince no longer sat in the open space before his tent to hear the pleading of his people and to give them justice. Instead, he gave authority to the elders and wise men of each tribe, that they should deal with every case, weighing it and dispensing justice, each according to his conscience.

'But if the merit on either side is such that not the weight of a feather can turn the balance, then the decision shall be mine,' he said. The people heard him and nodded; that was fair and reasonable, they thought. They began to discuss the arrangement among themselves, the elders puffed out with pride, their wives preening themselves, hands already cupped to accept small, secret bribes.

Moses had more to say; he raised his arms and the people were silent.

'Now I shall leave you for a little while. I go to speak with the god on the mountain where he first revealed himself to me, and there we will make again the covenant that was between him and your father, Abram. Let no man follow me lest he be consumed in the fire, for the wrath of this great spirit is terrible – have you not seen it yourselves in Egypt and on the borders of Egypt where Pharaoh's chariots sank beneath the waters of the Reed Sea where you, the chosen of Yahweh, crossed as though borne on the wings of eagles? So, I say, let no man follow me, or seek me among the crags. Eat, rest yourselves, and await my return. Aaron shall be your shepherd; if you are troubled, go to him.'

So he left them and there was not one among all the people who felt other than alone – suddenly alone and fearful in a strange place. An old woman, who had halted on her way from the well to hear the Prince speak, set down her pitcher and raised her voice in the long, sobbing lamentation of the bereaved; others joined her, putting dust on their heads and swaying backwards and forwards in an ecstasy of loss.

Zillah tugged at her mother's skirt and said, 'Mother, I think someone has died. Should you not mourn with these old women?'

'No one has died,' said Leah crossly. 'They are foolish old women who think that Prince Moses has gone for ever.'

'Has he?'

'*No*, child. He has gone up the mountain, that is all. And some people have nothing better to do than make a show about it – but that is not *our* way.' She clicked her tongue with impatience. 'Go, watch the goats, Naboth. See that they do not stray too far. And you, Zillah, what are you doing here? Go amongst the thorn-bushes and seek wool for me to tease into yarn. An idle child is an affront to heaven. Wait – take Micael's little ones – and do not let them tumble into the stream . . .'

To Ishvi she said, 'It is a great fuss about nothing. I shall be quite happy if the Egyptian *has* gone for ever; he has been a cause of trouble to our people since he first brought his shadow to the barley feast. I am glad to see him go !'

The days passed slowly. In the intolerable heat a little sickness broke out among the children; flies troubled them; the cattle grew thin again, with no will to search out the green places. Men grew lazy; there was nothing for them to do except gather the *manna* each morning, and even that became a burden. Hadad the Lame, who had lived well by usury in Goshen, grumbled more than any and tried to gather enough in one day to last for two. He stored it in two big earthenware pots and sealed the lids with wax but, when he opened them on the second day, there was nothing inside but worms and corruption.

The people scanned the steeps and gullies of the mountain for the sight of Moses and their eyes met only the emptiness of rock. A buzzard wheeled in the white sky, stooping and soaring. Lizards crept from holes in the ground and lay basking in the hot sun, their jewel-coloured eyes filmed and the pulse beating in their throats.

There were days when lightning cracked in the sky with a noise like a whiplash, and the earth quaked. Then Zillah and Naaman ran to the shelter of Leah's arms and huddled there, but Naboth stood in the open like a man.

'I am watching for Prince Moses' god,' he said. 'I am not afraid.'

'Prince Moses' god!' cried Leah. 'Prince Moses' god! Are there no other gods but this one?' The children fled from her rage; Ishvi caught them and they hid their faces against his chest.

'Hush!' he said. 'Hush, Leah, my own. It is the heat that has set such an edge to your tongue.'

'It is the stupidity of men,' said Leah. 'Listen. I am not one of those who protest that life was well enough under Pharaoh. For many it was evil, though for us it was not too hard. We were lucky; our children might have been lucky too. And perhaps, in the fullness of time, the condition of all our people might have bettered. Many of the Egyptians had kindly thoughts towards us; many of our own people bowed to the gods of Egypt. The lady, Isis, was a wife and a mother – we women understood her. We did not quarrel about gods. Then Prince Moses came – and suddenly everything is changed. We are free of that old bondage – I will not deny that – we are free to starve and thirst and die in a strange wilderness – but we die free people. So much has Prince Moses done for us . . .' Suddenly the rage left her and she stood, her hands hanging and her head bowed, tears coursing down her cheeks. 'Oh, Ishvi, beloved husband, what will become of us?'

Ishvi longed to comfort her, to assure her that it would be well with them all before long, that Canaan was but a short march away, but for once his tongue could not shape the soothing words. There was an emptiness in his own heart. He turned the children round to face her and said, 'Be good children. Do not let your mother weep!'

Zillah still clung to her father, making a stubborn mouth, but the small one, Naaman, who had only lately learned to walk upright on tottering legs, puckered his baby face and howled. They might have all wept together and found some renewal of hope beyond their tears, but at that moment Naboth appeared, his voice loud with excitement.

'Everyone is going towards Aaron's tent,' he shouted. 'Micael and Abirim and Dathan have gone by, and even old Hadad is almost running. The women are going too, leaving their pots on the fire to watch themselves. Will you go too? May I go? Come quickly or we shall be too late . . .'

'Come,' said Ishvi, holding out his hand to his wife, 'the people are taking their trouble to Aaron as Prince Moses bade them. It is all as it was in the old time . . .'

Leah dried her eyes on a corner of her shawl and lifted Naaman into her arms where he sobbed himself to sleep against her neck. 'It is nothing,' she said, and gave her free hand to Zillah, while Naboth ran before them.

There was a great crowd in front of Aaron's tent and many more people hastening towards it. Naboth wriggled his way to the front ranks but Ishvi and Leah stayed on the outer edge. The air was so still that, even there, they could hear all that was said.

Dathan cried, 'Aaron ben Amram, hear us! You were a

priest once, serving El, and our good was in your hands. All our lives we have known you and we have trusted you. We did not know Prince Moses as you knew him, but you trusted him and we followed you. Now he has left us and we are afraid. We do not know his god, what things anger him and what things are needed to placate him. We do not know how to pray to this god, we do not know his form. Therefore, son of Amram, we are afraid.'

Aaron spread his arms wide as though he would fold them all into his embrace, but he did not know what to say to them. Moses had been so long away that he, himself, had grown anxious.

'I am grateful for your trust,' he said, and waited.

Dathan shuffled his feet and continued. 'We do not know when Prince Moses will return – or *if* he will return. We have waited in silence, we have wasted our days in idleness and our nights are troubled by many fearful thoughts . . .'

'What would you have me do?'

'Lead us, Aaron,' said Micael. He was a simple man. He wanted no more than to get to Canaan, and that as soon as possible. He wanted to put down roots, make marriages for his sons, see his grandchildren grow up and, above all, he wanted a settled place in which to die. It was not much to ask.

'How can I lead you? Beside Prince Moses I am a child. His god does not speak in my heart. I do not know his plan for you . . .'

'Then make us other gods,' demanded Dathan, harshly. And the people murmured approval. Their voices rose to a clamour, 'Make us other gods! Make us other gods!'

Aaron raised his hand for silence. 'What you ask is not possible,' he said. 'A god is not something a man can make as he would make a pot from clay. It is not possible.'

But the people still cried, 'You are a priest. Give us a god we can understand and worship.' And some wept and others went down on their knees.

'In Egypt,' said Micael, 'there were gods of stone and wood. Have we not seen them carried through the streets on litters borne by priests? Were those not gods?'

'Those were but images of gods,' said Aaron with infinite patience. 'The gods resided in them at certain times and, in their carven shapes, spoke with the priests, even as the god of Moses spoke to him from the midst of a bush that burned. But these things in themselves are not gods any more than the stones that bruise our feet are gods, or the trees that shade us when we are weary.'

'Yet it is by their images that we know them,' insisted Dathan. 'Therefore make us an image of Prince Moses' god that we may worship him and, through our worship, understand.'

Then Aaron saw how he had stumbled into a trap of his own making. They are indeed children, he thought, and they are as bold and crafty as children. They have discovered that they have only to ask in a certain way and whatever they need will be given to them. Yet this is a very small thing they have set their hearts on. I will make them an image; then they will be glad once more and there will be no more contention.

'Bring me your gold,' he said. 'Bring me the gold arm-rings, and head-bands, the ear-rings and golden amulets the Egyptians gave you in their anxiety to see you gone. Bring me the gold you have gained by barter and saved from one generation to the next; bring it to me and I will make you an image of the god.'

Willing hands brought the fire to a white heat; even the smallest of the children helped, gathering dung for fuel. The women stripped themselves of gold ornaments they had treasured, the gifts of their mothers and their mothers' mothers, even the charms they wore to ease their birth-pangs. Gold ran from their fingers in a whispering shower, filling the coffer that was carried among them. Yet the crowd was smaller than it had been, for there were many who felt no need of an image to worship, and many who feared the wrath of the strange god whose servant, Moses, had brought nothing with him save a name and a command. Groups of people who had come to hear now scattered to their homes again.

Ishvi touched Leah's arm. 'We will not stay,' he said. 'This is a magic that does not speak to me here.' He touched his breast. 'It is not good to be present at the making of a god.'

Leah hesitated only a moment and then went with him. A part of her wanted to stay – so much that it was a physical pain in all her limbs to tear herself away from the place – but, in another part of herself, she was afraid. It seemed that she no longer knew the people about her though she had lived with them all her life; they had become like demons; their faces were like the faces of dogs and foxes, sharp and ravenous with eyes red and gleaming in the firelight. As she turned to follow her husband, a man caught her arm and thrust his face into hers, saying hoarsely, 'You are not leaving us? Wait! Already the gold melts in the vat. The god yearns towards his birth. He is like a child crying out in the womb . . .' His speech was slurred and his eyes wide and sightless; every hair on his head and in the tangle of his beard seemed to stand separate from the rest, outlined in blue fire. And Leah knew that this was her neighbour, Daniel, a quiet man who had carried water from the well when Adah, his wife, was sick, not minding the laughter of his brothers. This was Daniel and she shrank from him! 'Ishvi!' she called. 'Ishvi! Do not leave me here!'

Daniel shrugged and lumbered away. Leah ran, never stopping until she reached the tent, the safety of home. Ishvi left her there with Zillah and Naaman while he went back for

Naboth and Micael's children. Naboth wept at being taken away, digging his knuckles into his eyes and hanging back with his whole weight against his father's hand. Ishvi took his brother's children from the arms of a woman who stood by. In kindness she had lifted them, one straddling each broad hip that they might see the better, yet she did not notice when Ishvi took them away.

Aaron raised the vat of molten gold, and the people moaned. Old Hadad threw back his head and bayed like a dog howling down the moon. Gold poured from the vat held shoulder-high; it made an arc brighter than fire and fell hissing into the shallow basin of cold water prepared for it. Aaron stretched his hands, palms downward, above the water and closed his eyes. He felt the power descend through him; he felt it strong in the muscles of his arms, gathering in his hands, dropping from the tips of his fingers, shaping the gold in the likeness of the god.

The night of the Golden Calf – that was a time to remember! Torches flared in the space before Aaron's tent; the people danced and sang, throwing off their anxiety and tribulation with their travel-soiled garments, letting their bodies move freely in the firelight, the light of the god. Released, they leapt in the air, their limbs alternately contorted and spread-eagled; their muscles were like coiled springs as they bounded, agile as demons. The light was red and the stamping, leaping, perspiring bodies of the dancers were red, and the calf, glowing between the fires, was red too – red and gold like the very essence of fire.

Some of the people ran to their tents and brought out timbrels and tabors, little reedy pipes and stringed instruments to pluck with the fingers. Together they made music for the god; they wound ropes of leaves and grasses about his shining neck and set a crown between his sprouting horns.

'It is the calf of the great bull,' said Abirim. 'His father in the mountain has sent him to be our leader now that the Egyptian has left us. He will go before us into the promised land. He will trample our enemies in the dust; he will frisk with our cows in the green fields. Who will stand against him? Who will withstand his people, the people of the Bull?'

Aaron stood apart from them; he was very weary. The power that had passed through him in the making of the god had exhausted him. He could not stand alone and even the staff on which he leaned seemed too feeble a support for such a weight of weariness as was his. Also his soul was troubled. Miriam, the priestess who had danced in celebration of the Reed Sea crossing, stood at his shoulder, her eyes glittering like precious stones.

'Was this a part of the plan?' she asked, softly. And the ground stirred beneath their feet, the rock shifting and settling again. 'See, he comes!' Miriam pointed towards the mountain. Aaron narrowed his eyes but at first could see nothing, then – very small, very distant – a moving speck, light against the dark mass of cliff behind it. The sky paled. The tiny figure continued its descent, faster now. A cold shadow swept across the valley and light burst from behind the hills as the sun rose. In that moment, the flames surrounding the calf seemed to burn with black fire. The figure reached the lower slopes, assumed the shape of a man stooped beneath a burden of stone, and came on. The fires died.

Prince Moses had returned. On trembling legs Aaron went to meet him.

14

Ishvi said: 'Leah – keep the children close and do not go outside the tent. If neighbours come, make them welcome for kinship's sake, but guard your tongue and protect your ears from falsehood.'

His counsel was fair as always. Leah bowed to it and called the children to her side, to entertain them with stories until her husband should return. She took a pointed stick from the kindling and drew with it in the dry earth pictures of many strange and wonderful beasts – the crocodile with its gaping jaws, the wallowing hippopotamus and the baboon that sits among the rocks. The children laughed, for they were old enough to remember how the animals had looked in life, and surely they had been nothing like these of Leah's drawing. Thus the morning passed and Leah forgot to listen for sounds of anger and dispute from the camp outside; she no longer raised her eyes at every footfall, hoping it might be Ishvi's. She gave the children water to drink and curds to eat since no *manna* had been collected that day. They did not ask the reason but accepted with pleasure the fact that no day could be bad when stories were told in the morning; such a one had never been known before and might never be again.

Shortly after noon there came a visitor to the tent, Adah, the wife of that same Daniel who had frightened Leah the night before. Leah did not know her well but, like many others, had shared the burden of Adah's recent illness; she was glad to see her now, to learn from her the cause of the strange silence among the tents.

'Ah, Leah,' Adah said when the traditional greetings had

been exchanged, 'you are wise to stay in today. Such terrible things have been happening that a young woman's hair might turn white with the fearsomeness of it all, or her eyes be struck blind, or the milk dried in her breasts. There's many a one who rose yesterday a wife who will go to her couch this night a widow – and all because of the calf that Aaron made.'

Leah's eyes widened with horror. 'How so?'

'It was the Calf,' moaned Adah, and she rocked backwards and forwards, her veil thrown over her face to hide her tears. 'Such a brave, pretty young bull, he made the heart glad just to look upon him. And we made a smoke of offering for him, a few goats and sheep, and danced and made music. We were happy, Leah!'

'And now?'

'Then Prince Moses came. No one saw him come save Miriam and Aaron. They went to meet him but he brushed them aside. He had two great stones with him and, when he came to the place of the dance, he raised the stones above his head and flung them down among the people. Then he took the little bull and flung that down too. It was all smashed. His face was terrible and the people stood quiet, having nowhere to hide themselves from his anger.

' "I had brought you the law of Yahweh," he said, "the law that would set you apart from all other men, as the people the god had chosen. But you could not wait. You had to set up a false god and worship that!" '

'What then?'

'Eh, Leah! It did not seem like a false god to us. How should we know? But Prince Moses spurned the broken pieces with his foot and asked, "Was it this that brought you out of Egypt and across the Sea of Reeds, that sweetened the water of bitterness, and fed you with honey-bread in the desert?" We could not answer him – we are simple folk. We do not know about such things. Always someone has stood between us and the gods and showed us what to do. We stood quiet and waited.

'Then he turned to Hamor – your Ishvi's brother – and said, "Take your young men and go through the camp, and wherever you find those who gave worship to this – thing – kill! Though it be your brother, the son of your mother, *kill!*" '

Leah made a small, hiccupping sound and brought her cupped hand to her mouth. 'That Hamor! Oh, Adah, Adah! Micael was there. He was one of the men who persuaded Aaron to make the new god. I saw him – oh, Adah! May my eyes never look upon another thing. What did Hamor do?'

'He took his tall spear in his hand and went to do the Egyptian's bidding. I came away then. I could not watch while men put knives in their brothers' flesh. I looked for Daniel but I could not see him, so I came back alone. And to you, Leah, for company and comfort. For Daniel was there, and my four tall sons. Weep with me, Leah, for today Israel is a nation of widows.'

Leah put her arms about the woman's shoulders and held her close, murmuring to her as though she were a child. She felt true grief for Adah and her eyes dropped tears, yet her heart sang with thankfulness that Ishvi had turned his back on the Golden Calf.

'Ishvi will care for you,' she said softly. 'He is a good man and his shoulders are like those of an ox. No burden is too great for him, no task too hard. Did he not care for his father, old Kedemah? Do not his brother's children live in his shadow? Ishvi will care for you as though you were my sister.'

A little after this, Ishvi himself came in and seemed astonished to find Adah there, in his tent.

'What ails the woman?' he asked.

'Hush! She weeps for Daniel and her sons. Do not disturb

her in her sorrow. But for your wisdom, she and I would now be sisters in grief . . .'

Ishvi raised the woman from her knees and said, 'Adah, you weep too soon. Go to your tent. Daniel is waiting for you. Your sons have gone to comfort their own wives. So dry your tears and rejoice. Yahweh is merciful.'

Adah went, unbelieving, and Leah turned to Ishvi in amazement.

'She said that Hamor and his young spear-men had gone through the camp to kill. She said that Prince Moses ordered it in his rage, that Israel was a desolation of widows. Now you say otherwise. What is true? What is false?'

Ishvi put his arms round her and kissed her brow. 'It was so. In his first rage, the Prince said, "Kill!" But my brother Hamor was slow. And Aaron pleaded for the people, offering his own bared breast to the spear's point – and the Prince relented. The Calf he caused to be ground to powder and mingled with water in a great gourd. All those who took part in the celebration had to drink of it; it was a sin-eating. Next time they will remember the anger and the mercy and they will not fall so easily.'

'But why was it so wrong? This little thing they did . . . it has never been wrong before to make offerings and sing praises. How shall we know? How shall we ever know? In our houses we used to put the marks of our hands firm in the wet plaster of the walls, marks to keep away any spirits that might threaten our hearths – perhaps that, too, was wrong – but who is to tell us before we err? Shall we not sin first and be punished afterwards? And still not know? Ishvi – I am afraid!'

'You must not fear. Prince Moses stayed neither to eat nor sleep. He has gone again to the god in the mountain. Wait, my dove! He will give us a law by which we may order our lives . . .'

Leah pulled herself free from her husband's comforting arms

and stamped her foot in an ecstasy of rage. 'A law! So? Yet in Egypt we needed no law to hold us together. We lived simple lives, guided by kindness and tolerance, respecting our gods and the gods of others, our years measured by the seasons, lightened by festivals, each at its own time. But now we must be obedient to a god who does not speak directly to us, an El who is not the El we know. I think we have exchanged one bondage for another, husband, and I fear for the future of my children's children!'

If others felt as Leah did, at least they did not speak of it save, perhaps, in the privacy of their own tents. Indeed they spoke little on any subject, being chastened by their experience. They went about their daily lives in a dejected silence, waiting only for Prince Moses to return and take away the guilt he had laid upon their backs. This time they dared not think he might not return, as they had thought before, but a cloud of anxiety hung over them in all they did. Supposing the Egyptian should not prevail with this terrible, angry god of his . . .

And the days passed – morning, noon and evening. When the sun rose the *manna* lay upon the ground to be gathered in, and this surely was a sign that the god did not intend to leave them to fend for themselves. In fear and gratitude they gathered it, dividing it among their families, apprehensive at first that the god, in his displeasure, might turn it to ashes in their mouths, to poison in the mouths of their children . . . but it was not so. The honey-bread was as it had always been. So they took heart again and when the watchers at the edge of the camp cried out that their waiting was over – Prince Moses could already be seen, a moving mote against the high peaks – they rejoiced as a bride rejoices on hearing the steps of her bridegroom and, as the bride sweeps and garnishes her room, setting the best dishes before her husband, so did the people of Israel through all the camp, making a feast for his welcome.

Aaron, with the elders and chief men of the Tribes, made a journey of three days to bring him back. They met with him just above the place where the green humps of the foothills ended in rock and scrub, and when they came down again they were all solemn-faced and silent so that the people in the camp grew silent too, and put away the drums and tabors with which they had thought to play their leader in triumph to his tent.

'I will speak with you tomorrow,' said Prince Moses. 'Be you assembled together at first light, for I have much to say.'

Yet, weary as he was, he talked with Aaron long into the night, and Aaron pleaded with him for the people, for the old feasts that had sustained them in the days of their bondage, for the little gods who had cared for each family, easing their passage through the two dread portals that stand one at either end of every man's life, the gates of birth and death. Moses listened and rejected all.

'Let them keep, at least, their celebration of Tammuz,' said Aaron. 'Can they not worship your god in the grain, calling him by a name they know? What harm is there in that?'

'What harm was there in building a tower between the earth and the high heaven?' answered Moses. 'Yet it was not pleasing in the sight of the god. That is a tale from the ancient days of your own people, how they came from the east and founded a city in the plain of Shinar, and in the city began the building of a great tower, storey upon storey. The tower was never finished, Aaron, my brother, for the Great Spirit went among the people and confused their speech so that no man could understand his neighbour's words. How then could they work together in harmony? But *we* will be one people, with one tongue. And,' he added bluntly, 'there will be no more talk of Tammuz. Nor of any other god save Yahweh, He-who-is! Are we Egyptians that we should praise the sun for rising, or the moon for giving light to the darkness? Shall we worship the beasts we eat so that every meal becomes a ritual? Shall we burden ourselves with monstrous effigies and dance before them, mutilating our bodies with knives to honour Cybele? No, Aaron, and again no! In singleness shall be our strength – one god, one law, one people.'

'You will strain them too far,' said Aaron. 'It is beyond the power of man's mind to see beyond the many to the one . . .'

He would have added that the light the moon gave was not like that of the sun, that the barley-offering had its own rite and the sacrifice of flesh another, that each desert demon needed to be propitiated in his own fashion, but Moses interrupted him with a violent gesture.

'My god is a jealous god,' he said. 'He does not rule a host of little gods, each with his duty. All things stem from him, and he who sets up an altar to any other god belittles Yahweh. I am his mouth and you, Aaron, are his priest. Remember that.'

'I was the priest of Bull-El,' Aaron answered. 'You revealed his name, saying to us that Yahweh was the El of Abram – the great spirit our fathers knew. All my life I have served this god, yet there was also room for the gods of the hearth-place. Deny them these gods and the people will rise against you.'

'A divided people will not conquer Canaan.' Moses gripped Aaron's arm and shook him. But later he said, 'I will give them feasts, Aaron, that they may honour Yahweh as they honoured the gods of old. But there will be no more images.'

15

The Prince stood upon a rock to address the people, above them and apart, where he could be seen by all. Aaron, with his two eldest sons, stood near but below him and on his other side was Hamor, cloaked in a lion's pelt, his spear in his hand. In the shadow of the rock crouched Miriam the priestess, huddled in her dark garments, still and withdrawn so that her pale face seemed to float, disembodied, like the reflection of a face in a pool.

'Children of Israel,' Moses cried. 'Hear me – for I bring you the Law!' and his voice started echoes from the rocks . . . 'The Law . . . the Law . . .' rolling away into silence.

'How thin he is,' Adah whispered. 'He is burnt as dry as a stick. See how his belly is hollowed out like a cavern beneath his ribs . . .'

'Hush!' said Ishvi. 'Twice he has walked with Yahweh while we have waited here. Should a man speak with a god and not be changed?'

Moses spoke again and again his words were repeated all about in a dwindling echo.

'The Lord God, He-who-is, the great El of your father Abram, is a jealous god. He will suffer no other god among his people – not the god of the grain nor the gods of the hearth, neither the sun nor the moon nor any of the lesser lights he has set in the sky to guide you. You shall not worship any tree or spring or standing stone, for the god is not in any of these things; neither shall you make any image of the god, for his form is not known to any man and though you worship him with fire, he is not in that fire. Yet hear me! You shall not take the name of this mighty god and use it as an empty oath, for that way lies death. For six days of every seven you shall go about your work – but on the seventh day you shall rest. The seventh day shall be sacred to Yahweh who rested on the seventh day of his creation of the earth. You shall not lightly kill, for the mysteries of life and death are his only.'

The hard, commanding voice continued, speaking prohibition after prohibition, until the people fidgeted and looked anxiously at one another.

'This is a harder bondage than any I have known,' Daniel muttered behind his hand. 'What overseer in Egypt told me what I must believe?'

'Let no woman, having one husband, lie with another,' Moses said, 'for that is a sin against the hearth that is in her keeping and her punishment shall be stoning. And likewise let no man be tempted by a woman not his own – but let each family live in righteousness and virtue, honouring the parents and coveting nothing that belongs to another, lest covetousness should lead to theft, and theft to lies. Remember that the father of lies is Yahweh's enemy. Do not let him into the camp.'

'These are not harsh laws,' said Ishvi quietly to Daniel. 'These are such laws as we have always lived by, though it has never before been needful to set words round them.'

'Save the first of all,' growled Daniel. 'My mother worshipped at one shrine and my father at another, yet there was no discord between them.'

'You shall not want for rejoicing,' Moses continued in a more gentle voice. 'You shall keep the feast of unleavened bread in memory of your release from Egypt's tyranny. That shall be the great feast. And later, when the wilderness is behind us and the plains and fertile lands of Canaan yield to your husbandry, then shall two other feasts be kept, the feast of the harvest when the first-fruits of your toil bow to the sickle, and the feast of ingathering at the year's end when all is brought home and the fields lie empty beneath the stubble. These shall be your feasts to celebrate in thankfulness.'

'We are not in Canaan yet,' cried one, 'and there is still the wilderness to cross before we can speak of harvests.'

'And will the men of Canaan go meekly from their land that we may sow and reap?' demanded another. 'Surely they will turn us back and we will wander between the banks of the Jordan river and the Nile, until the end of time. What if they turn us back, Prince Moses?'

'What if they do?' asked Moses. 'Is our god not with us? He will make his people like spears in his hand, and the men of Canaan will go down before his might as did the warriors of Pharaoh in the Reed Sea. We do not travel alone, Yahweh goes with us. We will make an ark of acacia wood overlaid with gold and, when the time is right, the god shall enter it. Aye, the great spirit whose voice commands the stars and the seasons shall go with us into the wilderness and beyond.

'You, Bezalel ben Uri – and you, Oholiab, you are skilled in the working of metal and the setting of bright stones. Will you make such an ark?'

Two young men sprang forward from the crowd, their eyes alight with pride at being called to such a task. Soon others followed them, saying, 'Let us too bend our minds and our hands to making this house for the god to travel in.' And others passed a pannier round amongst the people as they had done before when gold was required for the Calf's making. But now it was not an image of the god they sought but a house that would hold the very essence of the god.

The days and months that followed were filled with heartening occupation as the ark took shape, carved and gilded, enriched with precious stones and enamelling, the last spoils from

Egypt. The women vied with each other to weave cloth for the hangings; to provide the thread, blue, purple and scarlet. Those with small skill in weaving twisted the loops that would suspend the curtains of the tent from clasps of bronze. The innermost curtains were of goat-hair, the outermost covering of tanned rams' skins and goatskins; the door was screened with an embroidered cloth stretched behind five pillars of acacia-wood, each overlaid with gold and set on a base of cast bronze.

There was no lack of will in the work, and no lack of pride. Whatever was done was perfect and Prince Moses, though he might fret himself to breaking-point at the obstinacy of his god's chosen people, could find no fault in their craftsmanship.

'You are happy now,' said Leah one evening when Ishvi came in from his work. She poured water over his dusty hands and served him with flat cakes and a cheese made from curdled goat's milk, soft-textured and with a strong flavour. 'It is good to see you happy and satisfied again!'

'I was made for work,' said Ishvi, drowsy with contentment. 'It is not enough for a man only to gather food from the ground, a crop he has neither sown nor tended, or to follow a flock of beasts from one resting-place to another. Man is a maker, Leah, before all things . . .'

'Or a destroyer?' Leah questioned, idly.

'No.' Ishvi shook his head. 'Men have destroyed much, and will again, but from fear or greed or anger. Freed from those dark passions, at peace with his spirit, man only makes.'

'He makes spears and knives. Then, armed to the teeth, he sets a watch on his neighbour's crops . . .'

'His neighbour's crops are ripened by the same sun, watered by the same rain. At peace with his neighbour, man makes a house for his god.'

With her sharp teeth Leah bit off the thread she was winding. 'My husband, you are the most trusting man that ever trod the earth. What if the neighbour's crops are sown on rocky soil? There are little white stones everywhere to blunt his reaping knife; he cannot cut his stalks close to the ground. The soil is thin as well as stony; the rain washes it down the hillside and leaves the roots exposed to the withering sun. This man will find it easier to gather spears than barley. I do not believe in your good fellowship.'

Lazily, Ishvi beckoned his wife to him and, when she knelt beside him, he took her chin in his hand and looked deep into her eyes. He sighed.

'Woman, there is neither trust nor belief in you. It was by no oversight that Zillah, alone of all the little girls, still wears gold rings in her ears. The others have given theirs to be melted that the god's house be suitably adorned – but not Zillah. That was your choosing.'

Leah moved away, letting Ishvi's hand fall. 'The other little girls may get more rings for their ears because their fathers are less trusting than Zillah's father. We do not get back what we give, Ishvi. Never in this life. Zillah's ear-rings were my mother's – they are a charm to preserve her sight. She has worn them since her first year and they are all the gold she has. Prince Moses' god has enough gold without Zillah's.'

This was a speech that saddened Ishvi but he said only, 'Perhaps you are right. Let my belief serve for us both.' Leah took his hand again and lifted it to her lips. 'Let my husband be no other than he is,' she said, 'but sometimes, beloved, my mind should be heard.'

She felt a need to warn him but it was of something she could not clearly see. 'I want to hold all that we have,' she cried fiercely. 'I want to hold it tight to me for ever and for ever. Do you remember the barley feast when we were wed? Your duty is first to me and to our children, and to your brother's children. Do not give what is our due to Moses.'

135

16

Twelve months passed before the tabernacle was finished and the journey resumed. In this time Prince Moses expanded the code of the law so that every smallest matter within the scope of a man's performance should be covered, from the manner of his sacrifice to the treatment of his slaves. Nothing was omitted. If any man were brought before his judges, for whatever reason, it was as though the Prince himself was present at his trial; the judgement was exact, the punishment pre-ordained, not subject to the bias of any individual nor fluctuating in justice according to a prevailing mood.

'That is good,' said Ishvi, but Leah merely shrugged and went about her work, refusing to argue. She could see the pattern of her parents' lives now shaping her own and Ishvi's. If she did not watch herself, she thought, she would grow like her mother, dominant, demanding. And Ishvi was like Zorah, so patient she could scream at him. True, Zorah and Rebekkah had been happy in their way but it was not a way that Leah wanted. A man must at least have the appearance of ruling, she believed, so when he praised Moses she was silent and when he went to make sacrifice at the horned altar before the Tent of Meeting, she sat dutifully at home.

She worried most about the children. In this rough and mountainous place they seemed to have grown wilder, freer. 'It is something in the air,' she said. 'I do not know what it is, but there is a change in them. They are obedient, they are respectful, they do their ordered tasks as thoroughly as any mother could wish . . . and yet . . . and yet . . .'

'They are too free,' Adah answered. 'The men spoil them.

They are for ever about the metal-workers' fires – helping, they call it – getting underfoot, *I* say. Or down on the plain watching Hamor schooling his warriors. That Hamor! He has said that every grown man should be skilled in war. The little boys hurl pointed sticks at a mark, and practice war-cries. It is not good for children to learn these things. It unsettles them.'

'Ah, but it is more than that. There is something in them that we never knew . . .'

'It is Hamor, I tell you! It is your husband's brother who has put his stamp on the children . . .'

Ah, that Hamor! He had caused nothing but trouble in his rebellious youth – but now he was a man and had power. Once people had said of him, 'That boy will come to a bad end!' yet he had prospered and now the grandchildren of those same people were like wax to be moulded in his hands. He was strong, he had wrestled with a desert lion to gain the pelt he wore; he was swift, even when armed he could outstrip the fleetest among them. He was solitary; men served him but no man called him friend.

Yet there came a time when they were glad of his strength and skill. Mount Horeb was behind them, the wilderness, apparently devoid of human life, all around. The Israelites marched openly in the order that Prince Moses had commanded, tribe by tribe, the precious ark in which the god rode carried in the midst by the Tribe of Levi, the Tribe of Judah leading, and the Tribe of Dan the rearguard of all. But the land was not as empty as it seemed. It was a violent, antagonistic country of parched soil and twisted thorns, boulders and prickly plants, yet it was as jealously owned as any fruitful orchard. It was the territory of the Amelekites, who watched, with mingled fear and anger, as the migrating hordes of Israel set out across their hereditary preserves. At first they did little more than watch, themselves unseen, hidden by rocks and the tangled scrub, moving as soundlessly as hunting cats, merging invisibly with the landscape but never further away from the invaders than the distance of a sling-shot. And the Israelites came on, rank after rank of them, a seemingly endless column of men, women and children, with their flocks and pack-beasts and their tents and household goods.

Now the watchers sent swift runners between their settlements to rouse the warriors who came from all sides to the attack, striking first at the very edges of the column, bringing down a man here and another there with arrows and slung stones. The Israelites might double their armed guards and double them again, but the Amelekites were always there, swifter than sight, killing with unerring aim and vanishing in the same moment.

It was time to stand. The men who had so often said, when they went reluctantly to be schooled in arms by Hamor and his Sons of the Bull, 'We are men of peace; we are not warriors!' now felt their hearts thrill to the battle-call. Eagerly they exchanged their staffs and shepherds' crooks for spears, and their domestic burdens for slings and satchels of stones. The women and children were sent apart with all the Tribe of Levi, Aaron's people who were ordained priests, for Aaron's sake, and therefore exempt from warlike service. Every other man of the age and strength to bear weapons went out to meet the Amelekites, and the battle was fierce and lasted for the whole of a day.

On raised ground above the battle-place Moses stood with his arms aloft in exultant communion with his god. He rejoiced to see his lazy, grumbling people so translated; their determination not to turn aside however great an army should come against them was in itself a victory. He would not fail them. Whenever they looked to him he would be there, willing them to overcome the enemy; he would be like one of those tall pillars of rock the first men worshipped, but flesh like themselves, flesh that wearied as they wearied, but which would not give in. He felt the lean sinews of his arms knot and shiver with the strain of holding such a posture. After many hours his sight dimmed and the earth seemed to reel beneath his feet, dipping and spinning away in a dark void – but that way lay defeat. As his arms dropped, the Amelekites pressed more fiercely and the Israelites were driven back. Seeing this, Aaron, together with a man called Hur who had gone to the rise with him, pushed a great stone behind Moses that he might lean against it and, one on either side, they held his arms steady until the trembling ceased. And the Israelites took heart again and drove the Amelekites before them until the sun set and the battle ended.

Hamor, with his bloodied spear still in his hand, went to the Prince and said, 'We are ready to march on Hebron, Lord. We will bridge Jordan river with the bodies of the slain. You have said truly that the god is with us.'

Behind him Miriam gave a low, mocking laugh as one who would ask, 'Whose slain?' but the Prince took Hamor's hand and said, 'By the god's will you have made warriors from bondsmen. It is a good beginning but it is not everything. We are too few to fight both Edom and Moab, yet we must cross their land. But first we will rest and bury our dead. When we reach the oasis of Kadesh, we will receive guidance concerning the way we must take.'

It was a great victory and a great loss. Many of the Israelites lay on the plain, their blood mingled with that of the Amelekites in a blending that was not of brotherhood. Fires burned all night about the field to light the mournful business of women seeking their husbands, lovers, sons; of warriors gathering weapons that would be needed again.

Here Micael found Leah and carried her back to his tent

where she lay without moving. She had thrown back her head-covering and her hair hung in tangles about her face. Micael smoothed it back from her brow, sad to feel it so harsh under his hands and to see the grey in it. Her cheeks were scored where, in her first grief, she had torn at her wretchedly living flesh. He took a cloth and washed away the dried blood, but she did not stir.

'Shall I not care for my brother's wife?' he said, and fetched the children to be with her. They stood in a frightened group, tall Naboth, Zillah who was too thin, her eyes too bright, and the little one, Naaman, his face crumpled with sleep and his thumb in his mouth. Micael's children were there also; they had long since forgotten their own mother, Sarai; their world was bounded by Leah, her scolding voice and unfailing love.

She spoke once only. She said, 'We were to have sat together at Naboth's fire.' Then she slept.

After many days she recovered, but the life had gone from her eyes and she became forgetful. The children grew wild, roaming where they willed, eating wherever they chanced to be when food was prepared. 'It does not matter,' the people told Micael. 'Let them stay. We are one family.'

The column formed again and moved on, Moses leading with Aaron and Miriam, and with them Joshua, the son of a Phoenician slave who had married into the Tribe of Ephraim. Joshua had been a beardless lad when the Tribes left Egypt; he was a youth still, but with a man's spirit. He complained at nothing, neither hunger nor thirst nor wounds, and he was a brave warrior. Moses trusted him as he would have trusted his own son, Gershom. But Gershom was a Midianite; Yahweh had called him to a different life.

The holy mountain lay far behind them, they had crossed the Wilderness of Paran; the Amelekites had seen their strength and fallen back to let them pass. They had survived. Now the oasis of Kadesh welcomed them with its groves of palms; they could set down the great, unwieldy ark and rest in the shade, knowing that their journey was near its end.

Prince Moses sent spies into the hills of the Negeb – Caleb, and Joshua, the most trusted. They returned after many days, bearing great bunches of grapes, of a size and sweetness the Israelites had never known.

'And not only grapes,' said Caleb, 'but everything is of a size that cannot be imagined – onions – cucumbers – garlic.' He laughed and made huge shapes in the air with his hands. 'Such growth! Why, Prince, there is something wanton in it . . .'

'And the men of the land?' asked Moses. Caleb's face fell.

'They, also, are giants,' he said. 'Huge, fierce men. Compared with these, the Amelekites are like children playing at manliness in sport. It will not be easy, Prince.'

'What says Joshua?'

'It will not be easy,' Joshua repeated, 'but it is not impossible, and surely men tire very quickly of what comes easily to them. These hill-tribes are a warrior people; they will not let us pass without battle. Of that I am sure. But *we* have the god with us, so what shall we fear?'

'Caleb?'

'It is for you to command. But, since you ask me, Prince, I say let the people have a voice in it, whether they go straightway against the hill-men, or whether they wait a while to gather their strength. For my part, now is the time. I have lost my heart to those rich hills and long to feel the springing grass beneath my feet again.'

'Aye. Now is the time!'

Then Prince Moses turned to the people. 'You have heard. So what say you? It is your battle, children of Yahweh – will you take it now, as Joshua and Caleb advise?'

But the people responded with sullen faces and they did not answer at once but muttered among themselves. Then one called, 'There were onions and garlic and cucumbers to be had in Egypt. We were not so hungry there as we have been since.' And another, 'You cannot pit hungry men against such giants as Caleb has described . . .'

The cry was taken up. 'No, Prince, we have had enough of your liberation, one way and another. We will stay here or turn about for Egypt!'

'Egypt! Egypt!'

Moses could have wept then. He looked from face to face and everywhere saw the same dull obstinacy, the same rejection. 'Dan?' he asked. 'Abimelech? Kohar? Benjamin?' But it was always the same. One or two shook their heads and looked ashamed, but none stood out to join the leaders.

'Very well,' said Moses. 'I cannot put fire in your bellies. Do what you will. But think first – I beg of you – and when you have thought, come to me.'

'What is decided?' asked Leah. 'Do they take up their spears again?'

But no one really knew. The men still argued round the fires, some saying one thing and some another. There was no pleasing them, Leah thought. First they had had to follow this god-intoxicated Egyptian wherever he chose to lead them, at whatever cost to their families, though they thirsted and starved, though they died in their hundreds. They were justified by the old traditions, they said, the old stories of Abram and Isaac and Ya'cob and Joseph, whose brothers had cast him into the well from which he had been resurrected by a caravan of traders and brought to Egypt . . . Joseph the twice-born, the reader of dreams, beloved of Pharaoh. Aye – such stories had fired the men as though they were tinder. But now they had learned that the tales could be neither eaten nor drunk and they cried that the old wells were dry, that the god was an empty dream, the promise an echo such as lingers in broken ruins and among tombs.

'What have gods to do with people?' she asked, following her own thoughts. 'Let them attend to their own work which is the ordering of the seasons, the bringing of rain. Let the gods leave us alone.'

Zillah came and sat at her mother's feet, her eyes huge in the thin face that was no longer quite a child's. 'What are you saying, mother? That Prince Moses was wrong?'

Leah shrugged. 'I say nothing. Prince Moses is a man. What he thinks is a man's business. His dreams are different from a woman's dreams. For Ishvi, your father, it was always enough, and therefore it is enough for me. But this I know – men die because of such dreams.'

'Then what will become of us?' Zillah put her head on her mother's lap, hiding her face. 'What will become of us?'

'If the men take up their spears and go into the hills, there will be widows in this camp where there are now wives. If the men decide to go back to Egypt, to the plenty they think they remember, there will be orphans where now there are families. There is death either way.'

She would not speak words of comfort she could not feel, but she laid her hand on her daughter's head in a brief caress. Zillah drew it down and held it against her cheek.

There was no more to be said between them but they might have sat for a while in a healing and companionable silence had not Naboth chosen that moment to burst into the tent, excitement flushing his face and making him forget his newly acquired dignity. Since his father's death he had struggled to be a man; now he was a boy again.

'They have agreed,' he said. 'It is all settled. Tomorrow we turn about for Egypt. Aaron will lead us so we need have no fear of losing ourselves in the waste . . .'

'Not hunger nor thirst nor the blistering sun nor bruising stones? Nothing at all to fear? That's fine news, son. What of the desert people? What of snakes?'

Naboth grinned down at her, thinking to himself that if it were left to women to manage the affairs of life, little enough would ever be done. They met every danger halfway along the road before they had properly set out.

'Snakes?' he said. 'The Lady Miriam will speak to the snake-goddess. And as for the rest – hunger and thirst and heat and stones are the lot of every man wherever he be. But Egypt is a land we know, not like this Canaan which we have never seen. We shall be safe again in Egypt . . .'

Leah stood up and cuffed his head, but with affection. 'What do you know of Egypt?' she teased him. But in that moment she was almost happy for it seemed to her that, in going back, it might be possible for them to unlive the experiences of the journey out, as though first Ishvi and then Sarai, Micael's wife, would rise from the dead to chide them for their griefs.

'I remember Egypt well,' said Zillah. 'You have told us stories about it, about the time when you were a little girl and Grandfather Zorah was alive. But even without the stories I would remember. I do not want to go back there, mother. I would rather see the new land beyond the hills where the giants live.'

And now that the decision was made, even those who had been most eager to return to the old oppression had become less certain. Preparations for the journey were but casual, begun and often interrupted. Men stood about and gossiped together like old grandmothers; they looked anxiously towards the Tent of Meeting, expecting a sign. They hesitated too long and their resolution melted away. They decided instead to attempt the hill road, whatever its dangers, and that too was the wrong decision.

For three days they assailed the hills, fighting valiantly, but they were routed. The hill-men, faces and bodies patterned with blue and ochre, descended in such numbers that it seemed impossible the hills could shelter so many, and they drove the warriors of Israel before them like frightened sheep while vultures circled the cloudless sky, waiting to drop on the feast of death below.

At Kadesh Barnea the people mourned again and were afraid. Moses had wanted them to fight. They had first refused, but later they *had* fought, and it had ended in defeat.

Aaron, Hamor and Joshua held council in Moses' tent. Hamor was for going again to the attack. 'There is nothing else we can do,' he said. 'It is for this that we left Egypt . . .'

Aaron could not agree. He had watched the men come limping back, supporting each other. He knew they would not go willingly into the hills again and would not be forced. Yet he had no alternative plan to offer. Joshua said nothing, but waited for Moses to command.

And Moses was silent. He waited for the god to speak in his head and the words of the others scarcely touched him. Hamor thrust himself forward, baring his teeth.

'We have fought and won; we have fought and lost. We can win again if the god goes with us. Tell the god *that* – and give the warriors a sign. But do not give them time to think. If we strike at all, it must be now!'

Aaron said, 'Prince Moses, they must rest . . .'

Moses looked from one to the other and saw only empty faces mouthing the shapes of words. Then the sound came and it was a meaningless crackling in his ears without any power to move him.

'You are both fools,' he said. 'Have I not told you often that the god *will* be obeyed – yet you continue to play with him. You would not do the god's bidding when the time was right; must he, then, wait on you, while your spirits blow hot and cold? How long, think you, will Yahweh suffer such treatment?'

'How can we know what is in the god's mind?' Aaron pleaded.

And Moses hissed, 'By listening, Aaron. By listening.'

He went out and called the people together. 'Yahweh is angry,' he told them, 'because you will not heed him. He is angry with me because I cannot make you hear. Therefore we shall do no good by staying where we are. We must be shaped to Yahweh's will, as metal is shaped in the fire. Now go and prepare yourselves, tomorrow we march towards the Reed Sea again, and in the desert will all the dross be burned away until we are a weapon fit for the god's hand to grasp.'

As Hamor listened his rage against Moses grew until he felt it would suffocate him. Each word that Moses spoke was a betrayal – a betrayal of all those who had followed him and fought for him, and a betrayal of Hamor who had trained an army for the Prince to lead. They had come to conquer Canaan; they had crossed a wilderness to do it – yet because they had lost one battle they must turn back.

Must they? Prince Moses was not the only leader. Had not he, Hamor, led men in Egypt – might he not do so again? He would put his power to the test.

When the Prince went back into his tent where Aaron and Joshua still waited, Hamor went among the people, speaking urgently.

'We were ill-prepared for that assault,' he said. 'We were not even of one mind. But were we to attack again, and soon, we should easily overcome these painted savages. They are drunk with victory. They will not expect us a second time after such a rout, therefore *now* is the time to strike!'

They were doubtful. 'You heard what Prince Moses said. Unless it be the god's will we can do nothing.'

'He has filled your bellies with falsehood so that you do not know what to believe. Were we not called Sons of the Bull in Egypt, before Prince Moses ever came amongst us? Has he ever claimed that this Yahweh of his was a different god to the El we knew? He has not – for we would not have followed a strange god. My brothers, rest well tonight, and tomorrow take up your slings and spears again; the El of our fathers will be with us . . .'

To many this seemed a reasonable argument and it needed very little more persuasion on his part before he had gathered the nucleus of an army. But it was not enough.

'We must depose this lying Egyptian,' said Hamor, 'and then the people will be more ready to do our bidding. When we say, "Go against these hill-men!" they will go. They need strong men to lead them, men of their own race, whom they can trust.'

With Dathan and Abirim, those two who had instigated the making of the Golden Calf, and with Korah of the Tribe of Levi, he went secretly to Moses' tent to bind him, and take over the governing of all the people. But Joshua stood as watchman and roused the Prince and rallied all the faithful to his side so that the whole camp was divided. And there were more who stood for Moses than for Hamor.

Thus Hamor's insurrection ended almost before it had begun. His desire for power and his will to destroy whatever lay in his path was turned against himself and he, together with his confederates, met death. Their tents and all their possessions were given to the fire.

'So Hamor has reached the end of *his* tale,' Micael said. 'Yet

147

it might have ended as sadly in Egypt. And sooner. He was always wild.'

'He was Kedemah's sorrow, as Ishvi was his joy,' said Leah. 'Now only you are left – you and your sons, and Ishvi's sons. Perhaps we shall all die in the desert and then Prince Moses' god will be sated.'

Micael spat to avert the evil such unlucky words might draw to the speaker. Then he began the preparations for the journey.

17

They went westward again, looking over their shoulders at the green palms of Kadesh Barnea and the fertile hills beyond. Their hearts were near to breaking but Moses spoke gently to them, telling them that Yahweh would have pity for them, that they need fear nothing. Were there not other ways into the land of Canaan?

Before long they were again in the region where *manna* fell, lying thick on the ground beneath the tamarisks, and knew that at least they would not hunger. So they went slowly, sometimes staying in one place for many moons, avoiding thought and avoiding contention. The children grew tall and hardy, tough as desert plants, capable as men but more single-minded. The boys carried slings almost as soon as they could walk unaided, and exchanged them for spears only a little later; even the girls took their turn at guard-duty so that the camp should not be surprised by night.

This new generation, thought Moses, was one made for the god's purpose. Born without memory, raised in freedom and toughened by hardship, these children were true inheritors of the promise.

He, too, longed to have sons of his own about him. Gershom and Eliazar he had put from his mind when, on Mount Horeb, he had sent them away with Zipporah, their mother. It was a lonely thing to serve a god, and leadership was a lonely thing. Aaron ben Amram had his wife and sons, and there was no fireside that did not welcome Joshua – yet Prince Moses, who carried the fate of the whole people, had no one. Truly he was never turned away; when he sat down with this family or that, the best that they had was offered him – but there was no freedom in their speech, their eyes shifted away from his. They were remembering the fate of Egypt's first-born, the Golden Calf, the death of Hamor the Rebel. How could they be comfortable in his presence?

He should have a hearth of his own but how could he take a wife from among the Tribes? It would be dangerous indeed to elevate one tribe above the rest, to found a dynasty on Judah or Benjamin or Dan, for whichever one he chose would set eleven others against him. Even with the god's help it was a risk he dared not court.

But what of the rest, the freed slaves and artisans who had left Egypt with them? They also were bound by the Law, as the Israelites were bound, but in gratitude, not as right. *They* would not boast of Prince Moses' favour or seek to climb by it ... and he would no longer be alone. Convinced of the rightness of this plan, Moses chose a wife for himself who was not of Israel but from the land of Cush – a woman with dark eyes and a soft voice. She had no family to jostle her, clamouring for position, ambitious to rule him and, through him, Israel. At last he could forget Zipporah; the tug of memory in his hands would sleep ...

Now they went south and east, making for the Sea of Aqaba and the gate of the King's Highway that would take them through Edom and Moab on a course as straight as an arrow's flight.

At peace with himself and with his dream fast approaching reality, he was hardly aware of the dissatisfaction of his people. He had become so used to the undertone of their grumbling that it was no more to him than the perpetual sighing of the wind through the ravines. They had suffered, let them complain if it eased them.

This time it was the *manna* that was the cause of their discontent. Their stomachs rejected its sweetness; their teeth ached for meat, however tough, however flavourless. They rose each morning thinking of meat – they talked of meat as the *manna* slid over their tongues. But they dared not kill the beasts, there were so few of them left.

They did not think of that earlier time when they had been fed from the sky until the day when the quails came again, exhausted from long hours of flying. The Israelites flung down their tents and burdens, and ran to net the falling birds, as many as they could before nightfall. They did not stop to make an ordered camp but raised their shelters anywhere and some did not bother even to do that, declaring that the sky was roof enough for any man. Nothing mattered save the thought of cooked food.

They ate until the skin was stretched tight across their bellies, and still they were not satisfied. The next day they ate again, and again the next. Everywhere disorder prevailed; the camp stank and the air was thick with flies yet the people were happier than they had been for many moons – until the sickness came. It was too late then to dig the pits, to arrange the tents with spaces between, to observe the innumerable, tedious laws of cleanliness.

The sickness went through the tents, touching here a child and there a man or woman. Many died and those who recovered were weak for many days. Zillah took it first and recovered. Micael seemed to rally and then sank again, falling into a stupor and then, almost imperceptibly, into death. Leah nursed them both and the sickness passed her by, though, having little to live for, she would have welcomed it. One by one she saw her generation fade and die.

Adah, the wife of Daniel, said, 'We have offended the god again. Let us go to Prince Moses and he will plead for us.' But

Leah would have none of it. 'Because of this strange god we have stripped ourselves bare to every evil,' she said. 'We have neglected the kindly spirits of our hearths who would have protected us. There is nothing we can do and nothing that the Prince can do. It were better for the jackals to eat us now, since we are doomed. Whether we die today or tomorrow is not important.'

But to Adah, who had never been strong and, for this reason, loved life all the more, it was important. With some of the other women she went to Miriam.

'Was it the quails?' asked one. 'Our bellies were sated with *manna*, with the sweetness. Was it the flesh we ate on the day of the quails?' But the others scoffed at her, saying, 'If that were so, would we not all be dead?'

'Lady,' they said, to Miriam, 'the god has breathed on your eyes, giving them sight beyond that of ours; he has quickened your tongue to speak. Will you go to Moses for us and tell him how the people mourn?'

Miriam sat in the shadow of her tent. She scratched in the dust at her feet and a little wind, blowing along the ground, scattered the sand again. She said, 'It is the woman from the land of Cush, the stranger Prince Moses has taken to his heart. It is for this marriage that the people suffer . . .'

The old women put their heads together and muttered. In their tattered garments they were like carrion birds seen at dusk. Miriam's heart yearned towards them for they had been young once, and comely.

'I will speak with him,' she said. 'Let him put this woman from him and all will be well.'

She halted the Prince as he came from the Tent of Meeting. His shoulders were bowed and he looked weary to the point of death for he had spent many days comforting the sick and mourning with the bereaved, but he stood patiently to hear

what she had to say. He had heard it all before, he thought, so
many times before. The few old men who represented the
Tribes ranged themselves behind him; the women clustered
together behind Miriam.

'Speak,' said Moses.

'I will not tell you again of the hardship of these people,'
said Miriam, 'for that you already know. I will not tell you
how they sicken and die, for so much your own eyes can
surely see . . .'

'For that I am grateful,' said Moses, 'but what, then, have
you to say, since you will not repeat what is obvious to all?'
and he drew his hand across his eyes. 'Be brief, Miriam.'

'I have this to say,' Miriam answered. 'I come to bid you
put aside the Cushite woman from your tent, because your
marriage with her is so displeasing to the god you profess to
serve that he vents his anger upon the people, sending hunger
and thirst and plague to torment them . . .'

'What god says this?'

'I have spoken with the wind and the wind told me. But
look into your heart, Prince, and dare to tell me it is not true.
The woman is not of our race, the elect of Yahweh. She has
not shared our burden, the command of Yahweh. She has en-
snared you with a dark magic we do not know. Put her away,
Prince Moses, that the people may live.'

Moses let out his held breath in a long hiss. 'I do not know
the god who spoke to you in the wind, but I will answer him.
A multitude of races came with me out of Egypt – Israelites
and Cushites and even men from the far sea-coast where the
gods wear tails like fishes – but they were one people, united
in that they were oppressed and looked for freedom, that they
were willing to follow me and trust in the might of my god.
We have suffered together and many of us have died. I mourn
with you. I weep with you. Before Yahweh, who has heard

153

your complaining voices and stayed his hand because I have pleaded for you, before Yahweh I tell you that I love this obstinate, proud and insatiate people. I would give my own life for you – but I will not put aside my gentle wife because an unknown god requires it!'

He turned away but Miriam darted across his path and held him by the sleeve.

'Are not the daughters of Israel fair? If the Lord Moses needs a wife to comfort his nights let him choose from the maidens of the Tribes. Or does the Prince of Egypt abhor the flesh of Israel?' she spat at him. 'Oh, Prince, does your dark Egyptian heart still lust after darkness? Perhaps that is why you keep us so long in the desert, that we shall all burn in this everlasting sun until even we are as black as the men from Kemt who were your fan-bearers in Egypt.'

'Have a care, Miriam. It is the serpent who speaks with your tongue.'

'I do not fear the serpent. It is not so long since you, yourself, raised a serpent on your staff, when the people were sick from stings. Have you forgotten that?'

'It was Yahweh who wrought the cure. The serpents were sent by the Mother, the Lady of Snakes. I made of her a gift to the Father. He accepted the offering and the people were troubled no more. Go back to your tent, Miriam, and we will forget all this foolish talk.'

'Foolish?' cried Miriam. 'It is you who are the fool, or worse, for you cast aside a whole people as though they were nothing, for the sake of a pair of dark eyes in a dark face. You have forbidden us our gods and now you think nothing of offending your own. But hear this, Prince Moses. We will not perish with you when your god flings you down. We will wrest your leadership from you and send you away, you with your night-hued concubine. Then you will see what sort of luck she brings you!'

Miriam took a step forward and raised her hand accusingly. Moses did nothing. He simply looked at her. She wavered and stood still, her hand outstretched before her eyes. She moved her fingers convulsively, then spread her other hand, turning it about. For what seemed a very long time she stood like this, gazing at her hands, then she covered her face with them and moaned, crouching low on the ground.

'It is leprosy,' she whispered, and though her voice was scarcely audible, those nearest to her took up the word and soon it spread like fire through the camp. Leprosy. Miriam has leprosy.

Then there was a long silence. Aaron touched Moses' arm and said, 'Pity her. I also have despised the Cushite woman.' Moses did not answer and Aaron said again, 'Pity her. It is a very little sin for such a punishment. Do not imprison this living woman in dead flesh that is already half eaten away. Heal her, Prince Moses. I beg you, heal her.'

But Moses shook his head. 'It is as the god wills. If a woman so offends her father that he must spit in her face to silence her, shall she not be shamed seven days? Miriam, take your leprosy outside the camp until seven days have passed . . .'

The women made a wide path for her and she went away, cowering, her hands still hiding her face. Some said they saw no mark of the disease on her, neither on her hands nor on her face before she had hidden it. 'Her flesh was as whole as mine, I swear it,' said Adah, but others were less certain and no one could deny that Miriam herself had seen the dreaded whiteness; so much the shock in her eyes had testified.

When the seven days had passed, Miriam was brought again to the Tent of Meeting and Moses lifted the veil from her face. 'Give thanks to Yahweh,' he said, 'for your skin is clear again. You are cured.'

To the assembled people he said, 'The god has punished this woman because she raised her voice against me but, to show his mercy, he has made her whole again. Be chastened by the lesson and remember it, for we are in his hand.'

He was very patient with them though his weariness was now so great that even speech was difficult. The constant set-backs and disappointments, the unceasing complaints, the skirmishes, deaths and plagues, had all contributed to wear down his first high optimism. A tic beat below the skin of his cheek, and now and again a convulsive shivering took him so that he had to clench his teeth to stop their chattering. Sometimes he even doubted the strength of his relationship with the god.

'It was not the quails,' he said. 'Yahweh knows well that men must eat. It was your gluttony that brought the sickness; it was because you were so mad to eat that you neglected the laws made for your protection. Another time you will remember.'

18

The city of Ezion Geber squatted at the northernmost shore of the Sea of Aqaba. It was an ugly and forbidding place; smoke from the great copper refineries hung low above the rooftops and poisoned the air; even the free workmen looked like slaves.

Darkness had fallen and the great gates were closed. The Israelites would have made camp there, in the shadow of the wall, but the fumes of the smelting were intolerable to their desert-cleansed lungs and they moved further along the coast to rest at the very edge of the sea. That night, for the first time in many moons, they made music; the King's Highway lay only a day's march beyond the city and the worst of their journey was over.

The children ran freely along the shore, gathering shells and marvelling to find so many, breaking off branches of the brittle white coral that seemed to them to be strange trees springing from the sand. The salt air stung their eyes but it was a small discomfort compared with what they had endured, it did not spoil their play.

Naaman did not forget his mother. He brought her the biggest shells he could find, as many as he could carry, and poured them into her lap, hoping to make her smile with him again. For a moment Leah's hands strayed among them but not even their unfamiliar beauty could hold her long. In her imagination she walked on the beach with Ishvi and listened while he pointed out the stars and told her what names they had and which spirits ruled them. Naaman's gifts lay forgotten, but he had not really expected more. Carefully he collected them all together once again and took them to the Lord Joshua who found time to admire each one.

The next day Moses sent envoys to the King of Edom. It was as well, he thought, to ask permission to travel the King's Highway. He did not think at all that the permission would be refused.

But it was refused. The King of Edom had learned from his spies of the Israelites' approach; he knew their condition and their numbers and he would not allow such a vast horde of hungry and desperate people through his land.

'We will not wander from the road,' the envoys assured him. 'If we touch even one blade of grass, drink as much water as can be held in a child's cupped hands, we will pay for it. You will not lose by our crossing.'

'Pay for it?' scoffed the King. 'What use would your skeleton beasts be among my own fat cattle? I do not need such payment as you could make. And you shall not cross my land.'

To his headmen he said, 'Take a score or so of fresh young warriors and let them shake their spears a little at these arrogant beggars who sit outside my gate; they will soon scuttle back to the hills.'

There was no argument that could prevail against him. With long faces the envoys went back to Moses and gave him the King's answer.

'That is not the only way into the land of Canaan,' Moses said, but his voice sounded hollow, even to his own ears, and the tic beat so strongly in his cheek that his whole face fell awry.

One night more they stayed by the shore of Aqaba but had little rest from it. From sunset till dawn the warriors of Edom circled the camp, rattling their spear-sticks and yelping like wild dogs. The next day they set out north again through the valley of Arabah and the Edomites harried them all the way until, for fear of them, the Israelites turned away through a gap in the hills into the wilderness of Zin, skirting the Negeb, and down again to the wilderness of Paran, the country of the Amelekites.

The desert was without pity and without end. The land and the seasons span together, tricking memory, robbing the mind of its ability to select and register so that, looking back, no one knew how many times the wild tribesmen, the Amelekites, had been fought and overcome. Perhaps once only, perhaps a score of times. Between the clamorous urgency of each first trumpet-call and the silence of the following dawn when nothing moved save for the glutted vultures, too heavy still for their great wings to lift, a thousand lives were lived and died.

It was a time of bitter wandering, circling the waste, turning about and round again and up and down until it seemed that only the stars changed. Surely this rocky defile had engulfed the people once before? But long ago in the spring of the year when the narrow strip of sky above the purple-shadowed rocks had been blue. They had been glad of the sudden, striking cold as they left the sun outside to burn up the plain behind them. Their feet had known these hills through many seasons – when the earth was parched, cracking under the white heat; the thorns, dead brittle wood; the streams dry and choked with stones; and again when the land was awash with green and every bush a riot of flowers. Yet they were the same hills . . . and their ghosts would wander there until the end of time.

The wilderness was peopled with ghosts – driving shadowy beasts, fighting insubstantial battles, going to and fro among the living, lying down with them at night and going on with them each morning. Who, unless he had more than human sight, could tell the living from the dead?

Leah could not tell. She was ever searching among the dead for one beloved shape, hearing again the groans of the dying and the wailing of the bereaved, raising a head here, turning a dead face to the torchlight . . . yet surely it was a dream, for the battle still raged and Prince Moses still stood apart on his little eminence, upright as the rock behind him, his arms raised and the sun going down in fire. That was a picture Leah's mind held intact, formed between the unclenching of her hands and the beginning of her scream when she had found Ishvi in the deepening dusk, and the sound and the picture ran together so that her memory of the whole day was accompanied by the thin, high sound of her keening voice and the day itself began with the death of its ending.

Heat and weariness and thirst – these three things made the pattern of their lives. Weariness, thirst and heat. Thirst – thirst – thirst. Bruised feet might rest a while, the night gave ease from the sun's burning – but thirst knew nothing of night or day, it knew no rest. It was crueller than hunger; it was sharper than the memory of the whips Pharaoh's overseers had wielded. The people marched slowly and yet more slowly; each day they covered a smaller distance. The ark of the god lurched in their midst, carried by men who felt its weight more heavy than its sacredness. The god was a burden they could not set down. And they dared not raise their voices against the god for this was the Great Spirit who had overturned Pharaoh's chariots, who had destroyed the prancing calf Aaron had made for them in the foothills of Sinai – it was death to speak against such a god as this.

Prince Moses' eyes devoured the desert, the rise and fall of the land in its never-ending flow, red and accursed. His tongue rasped over his dry lips and the blood throbbed behind his eyes.

'God of Abram!' he cried. 'God of Isaac and Ya'cob and Joseph, hear these people. They thirst. Give them water. Lord of the Heavens, send rain over this dead land . . .'

No land is dead, whispered the voice in his secret being. There is no desert that does not flower when the time is right. Are there not waters under the earth, under the very rocks and stones? Shall the creeping things of the waste places drink while my own chosen people wither and die?

A tiny lizard darted from the shade of a stone. No longer than a man's finger, it glowed like burnished copper, like a bright thread of metal. It stood for a moment, dazed in the white noon-light, then zig-zagged across Moses' path to vanish through the crevice of a rock. Moses watched it go. In his mind he followed it down a labyrinth of branching ways, the hollow veins that laced the stone. Its questing nostrils led it down through the cool dark to the place where water lay, pure and cold. There, far below the surface of the earth, it drank.

Moses screamed and struck the rock. Again and again he struck it – though the water, released by the power he had embraced on Sinai, gushed unnoticed at his feet. Joshua went to him and led him away while the people, following Aaron, filled their water-carriers and slaked their thirst.

When Aaron went at last to the Prince's tent he found him sitting in an attitude of despair, his face hidden in his arms.

'There is no shame,' said Aaron quietly. 'The god gave you more responsibility than any man can carry. There is no shame in breaking. And you gave the people water.'

'I gave them *nothing*,' said Moses. 'The water was there, I had only to ask the rock to yield it – but I did not ask. I commanded. I struck the rock as though it were my enemy; I forced what would have been freely given. I usurped the god's right . . .'

'Our need was great. Because of what you did, our need is no more.'

'I am shamed before the god,' said Moses, and he shrank into himself, a lonely man. 'This place shall be called Meribah, the waters of bitterness, because my heart is bitter that I have broken my faith . . .'

Aaron dropped to his knees and raised Moses' head to look at him. But Moses flung aside his hand and cried, 'The transgression is not important. Though I sinned a thousand, thousand times, do you think this god would not forgive me? Did he condemn those who made the Golden Calf? Did he destroy *them*? I tell you, Aaron, Yahweh is like no other god . . .' and then, as though speaking to himself, 'Who shall say what he is? A pillar of cloud, a voice in the fire, a bellowing from the dark centre of a storm? He speaks in my belly and I obey. I feel his power gather like a knot in my breast and then, for me, there is no sound in all the air but the sound of his voice. Until today I have been a true mediator between my god and his people – but today I neither listened nor obeyed and, by all the laws of all the gods, the power should leave me now. But it is still with me, Aaron, and I am afraid.'

'You were charged to lead these people into Canaan,' Aaron said. 'Until you have done that, you cannot be released.'

'*These* people?' Moses laughed abruptly. 'Aaron, my brother, not one of these people will enter Canaan, not one of all the multitude I brought away from Egypt – except the children and a very few others, perhaps, those whose hearts are without pride. Have the people deserved Canaan? Have they earned it? I thought to make warriors of them, with Hamor's aid, for we shall need warriors when we go against the cities – but Hamor had too much pride and is dead because of it . . .'

'Prince Moses,' said Aaron, carefully. 'I have served you well. Even when I have not understood, I have trusted and followed you. I have given my sons to be priests before your god. When the people feared, I comforted them, making promises in your name. What shall I tell them now? That you have led them into death? That you have abandoned them because they are not warriors?'

Yet even as he spoke he knew in his heart that it was true, what Moses said. These people could not conquer Canaan. They might stand firm enough against the undisciplined fighters of the desert people who came against them – but these were little skirmishes. It was not warfare. Between whiles the men forgot what Hamor had tried to teach them, they carried their spears clumsily, they had no care for weapons at all.

'What shall I say to them?' he asked again.

Anger flared again in Moses' eyes and he shouted, 'Tell them what you will. Tell them nothing. Or tell them – if you like – that it is because of the Golden Calf. For that is true, in its way. In the Calf the weakness of their purpose was first manifested. And weak men will not take cities . . .'

Aaron flinched.

'Or,' said Moses, 'if your stomach is too delicate to share that burden with them, you who made the Calf, tell them it is because they would not dare the Negeb though the god was with them.

'Or tell them nothing!'

Aaron left him then. He did not hear the Prince add, 'It is for me too – this ban. Not even I shall enter the land of the promise, for their weakness is also mine . . .'

19

Zillah bloomed into sudden beauty. It was as though she lay down one night a child and rose the next day a young woman, ready for marriage. The ground before Leah's tent was trodden firm by the procession of stripling warriors suing for her hand, but Leah's mind had gone away into the shadows where Ishvi waited. To each she answered, 'You must ask my husband. It is not for me to bestow our daughter.'

Micael might have reasoned with her or, himself, stood in Ishvi's place to choose a husband for Zillah – but Micael was dead. And Naboth, Ishvi's eldest son, was a child still as Leah saw him; his word counted for nothing.

The procession of young men thinned and Zillah, unwed, felt her beauty fade. Now, when the Tribes gathered for the small feasts of thanksgiving that Moses allowed them, she sat with the old women rather than with the maidens whose promise rivalled and then surpassed her own. They were free to marry, she was not. Seeing her friends go laughing, one by one, into the mystery her mother's grief denied her, she resolved at last to defy Leah and marry without her blessing. It was a bold step and not to be taken without consideration but, to the new generation bred in the desert and knowing a freedom their parents had never known, it was not impossible. But by that time it was too late. The young men no longer stooped beneath the fringe of Leah's tent to ask for Zillah's hand. 'Yes, she is beautiful,' they told each other, 'but what man can wait for a ghost to answer him?' and they did not speak their minds to Zillah, who would have married any one of them though it estrange her from her mother for ever.

In despair she went to Miriam.

'Help me to a husband, Lady,' she whispered. 'There is no other help for me in all the world . . .'

Miriam had declined sadly since the day she had raised her voice against Moses at the Tent of Meeting and, her power waning, she received few suppliants from among the women. The young ones managed their lives so differently – and what need had they of a barley queen here in the desert? Tammuz had died long ago and no one now danced the ritual of his rebirth; in this red landscape there was no grain to celebrate. And Yahweh, for whom she had danced the triumph of the Reed Sea crossing, had rejected her, humiliating her before all the people.

Yet here was Zillah, the daughter of Leah who was the daughter of Rebekkah, kneeling to her in the dust even as an earlier generation of maidens had knelt to the Old Grandmother. She felt a glow of satisfaction warm her and she reached out to the need in the younger woman's voice as though to a fire.

'Help me,' said Zillah again, 'for there is no one else to advise me . . .'

'Help you? I – an old woman despised by the god? How can I help you?'

'You know how it is with me . . .' Zillah put aside her veil. The moon was kinder to her than the sun, bleaching her parched skin to fairness and gentling the cruel hollows of her cheeks. 'I am not yet old – but what man will look at me unless you give me a charm to turn his eyes in my direction?'

'I have no charms to give,' said Miriam. 'The god has stolen away all my old magic and left me empty and useless as a leaky pot thrown on a midden. For help you must go to the Mother.'

Zillah licked her dry lips. 'And how shall I find her in this great waste?'

'That is not hard. Less than a day's journey towards the place where the sun rises, there is a little spring and a grove of trees sacred to her worship. Go there alone, purify yourself in the water, and wait –'

'Alone?'

'Alone.' Miriam's voice in the darkness was soft as breath. 'Make your offering to the Mother and take the man she sends. It is what all maidens did in the ancient times. She will hear you as she heard them.'

It was a fearful thought. Zillah's hands grew numb and her body jerked with the violent thudding of her heart. 'What of Yahweh? He has forbidden us to traffic with other gods.'

Miriam spat her contempt. 'What does a great stamping bull know of maidens? What has he done for the women of Israel save make widows of them? Had your father lived it might have been different for you – but Ishvi ben Kedemah is dead and your own mother's mind is shrouded in the mists that separate the quick from the dead. Who is to help you gain a husband unless it be the Mother of all living things?'

'I cannot do it,' said Zillah. 'It were better that I defied my mother in the sunlight . . .'

'Perhaps so. But how many young men have called at your tent in recent times?'

'Better I die a maid than offend the god . . .'

'There are too many withered branches on the tree of Israel and each, in its own way, is an offence to the god. If he sends rain for the thirsty roots to drink so that the sap rises to make the leaves unfurl their green, who shall dare to blast the fruit in the bud? That is a high matter for two women to whisper about in the night, Zillah. You came to me with a question heavy in your heart and I have answered you – but it is not for me to choose the way you will go.'

Still Zillah hesitated. Far out on the plain below a wild dog howled to the pack. Miriam sighed. 'Only you can choose,' she said, wearily. 'But I will tell you this, that your choice was written in the stars long ago, before your father and mother met at the barley feast – long before that. What you think you are choosing is not so important after all. We are in the hands of the Mother, Zillah. She is the womb and the grave; she brings forth men and gods and they play for a while in the world, till she calls them home again.'

Ah, thought Zillah, if this is so then even Yahweh, the jealous one, must acknowledge the Mother. 'I will go,' she said, resolutely. And behind her veil, Miriam smiled.

Less than a day's journey, Miriam had said but, though Zillah started early, it was already dusk before she reached the grove.

It was a desolate place. Wandering people still called it the Well of the Lady for it had indeed been a celebrated shrine in the days when their grandfathers were young. Then the spring had bubbled clear from the rock, creating a green oasis in the burning land; now the old channel was choked with fallen masonry and the water oozed and spread along the ground in shallow, weedy pools beneath overhanging branches. Snakes still bred there, protected by the Lady of Serpents, and wild dogs came at night to drink. At certain seasons migrating birds alighted in the trees but, for the most part, the Lady dwelt in solitude.

Stepping fearfully between the puddled hollows Zillah came at last to the great stone in the centre of the grove. Trees shut away the fast fading daylight; there was no wind to rustle the leaves and break the deep silence. Shivering, she knelt before the stone, her hands empty of gifts and only a very little hope in her heart.

'Lady,' she said, 'help me, for you understand the needs of

women. Let me not grow old without love. Let me have children to comfort my age when the years are behind me . . .'

She crept closer and put her face against the rough stone. 'Mother of beasts and men and all living things, hear me!' The stone face, stained with lichen, gazed into the trees.

Pebbles clattered behind her and Zillah whirled round, terror constricting the muscles of her throat. Until that moment she had believed in the power of the Mother with only part of her mind, now she believed entirely and was afraid.

A man was entering the Mother's sanctuary; the hem of his long outer garment stirred the scummy water but he paid no heed, walking in a direct line to where Zillah crouched at the feet of the stone figure.

'Who is there?' Zillah's voice was a dry croak. She reached back with her hands to touch the ancient rock, seeking re-assurance – but could the Mother protect her from her own wish? She had asked and the Mother had heard her. That must be the end.

'You know me, Zillah . . .'

Uncertainly Zillah peered into the dark.

'I am Baal-Shazzur . . .'

Ah! Baal-Shazzur – the maker of pots. Indeed she knew him. He had been a slave in Egypt, one of those who had followed the Hebrew people into freedom. As a child, she had watched him at his craft as they rested on the lower slopes of Mount Horeb, so long ago. He'd made her a little dish with a grasshopper painted on it, so cleverly done and all in one brisk line. 'That is your mark,' he'd said, 'your own sign for the first letter of your name, Zillah, so that everyone will know it is yours.'

Relief made her laugh, and then she remembered the serious-ness of her mission.

'You must go away,' she said, sharply. 'My business is with the Mother!'

'Mine too, perhaps.' He stooped beneath a low bough and came on. 'Would you deny me entrance to her shrine when I too have come so far?'

'I was here before you. You must wait for another time . . .'

'Tonight the moon's disc rises exactly above her brow. When such a night comes round again we will be far away. This is the time of all times most favourable to the Lady's worship . . . the stars have told me so.'

'You followed me,' Zillah cried. 'It is obvious, so do not talk of the stars to me. I have nothing to say to you – except go!'

Baal-Shazzur seated himself on a fallen pillar. 'I followed you,' he agreed. 'And now I would give thanks to the Mother, for she has led me by the hand as though I were a child.'

Zillah stamped her foot. 'You have spoiled it,' she said. 'So *I* will go, if you won't!'

'Not yet,' Baal-Shazzur said. 'We must be honest with each other, you and I, for I am too old to play at courtship and you are too solemn. No, Zillah, those pretty games are for others, whose need is surely less great than ours . . .'

'I do not understand you,' said Zillah, but she understood well enough.

Baal-Shazzur sighed and looked away. 'You came tonight to hang up your girdle to the goddess – to take the man she sent you. Suppose I am that man? Did not she, who knows all things, rouse me from sleep as you went past my tent, so that I should follow?'

Zillah listened in dismay. This man was old – he had been grown while she was still a small girl hugging a wooden doll and her mind starry with make-believe. Baal-Shazzur was a good man, she would not deny it, but his face was lined and weary, there was already white in his beard . . .

The expression in her eyes hurt him as though a knife had been plunged into his belly but he would not show his pain.

'Come, it is not that bad,' he said. 'Did you think the Lady might have given you her own husband, the Moon-god, for your lover? Ah, not in your heart, Zillah! Better old Baal-Shazzur, the maker of pots – the maker of *beautiful* pots – ' he corrected himself, 'than some wandering tribesman from without the Law.'

'I did not think – ' Zillah began.

'You thought enough. It is a long day's walking over rough ground between the camp and this shrine. If you did not think before, you had time enough to think then. Make the best of it, Zillah. I promise you I will be a good husband to you.'

Zillah put her hands to her burning cheeks. 'I am ashamed,' she said. 'It was cruel of me to speak so but truly I did not think. Not in the beginning or during all the day except that I wanted children of my own and that the Lady would provide for me. I had prepared my heart to welcome a stranger, but beyond the journey and the asking I did not look. You are indeed right and I am wrong. Friend or stranger, I must take whom the Lady sends and be glad.' Her voice shook. 'She might have arranged it more simply, I think, and saved us both a long and tedious walk.'

'You think I should have spoken instead to Leah, your mother? And what better answer would I have had from her than had Benni, the son of Hamiel? Or Laban the younger? Or Nahor? "You must ask Ishvi. It is not for me to give my daughter." Isn't that what she always said? I am too old to wait, too determined on one woman only – I could not look elsewhere for a wife. What other course for me than to ask the Mother of all living things?'

'Did the witch, Miriam, tell you she had sent me here?'

'She did not. I have told you, Zillah, the Mother roused me

as you passed my tent. But I had already made this journey once. Did you not see?'

At the base of the stone, half-hidden in the coarse grass, was a little pot of baked clay, its sides scored with a pattern of running deer. Zillah knelt and parted the grass. The pot was so small it might be held in her cupped hands and it was half-filled with grain.

'I also brought a gift,' said Baal-Shazzur.

For a while there was nothing more to say. A snake slid through the reeds and into the water; outside in the moon-washed waste a dog howled and was answered by another and then another.

At last Baal-Shazzur said, 'Look at me, Zillah. If you wish, I will ask the Lady to release you from your vow. Perhaps you spoke truly when you said you had not thought and I would not hold you to a plan shaped when your mind was not in it. Also I have been a slave, a man who is owned like a beast and may be bought and sold or given or gambled away – I do not complain of that for it was as a slave that I learned my craft – but I know well that a free-born woman might feel shame in such a marriage. If it is thus with you, answer me now and I will be your guide and protector across the desert until we reach your mother's tent and after that I will never trouble you again.'

It is more than I deserve, thought Zillah, but indeed I cannot marry this man. She searched her mind for words that would soften the refusal and as she hesitated the Mother worked her magic. Zillah looked again at the potter she had known all her life and, though the moon silvered his hair even where time had not touched it, and darkened the lines in his cheeks, he no longer seemed to her like an old man. She touched his wrists where the blood throbbed and said, 'I will marry you, Baal-Shazzur, and not only because you are the man the Mother sent, and not only because you are wise and patient nor because of the dish you made me once, long ago, with the grasshopper on it – though all those things are a part of it. I do not understand but I am quite sure . . .'

When the sun rose Zillah took off her golden ear-rings and hid them in the grain Baal-Shazzur had brought. Together they left the shrine and set out on the long walk back to the Israelites' camp.

'Tell me about your people,' Zillah said. 'My life you know already, but yours is a mystery to me.'

'That is a long story,' said Baal-Shazzur, 'and where shall it begin?'

'At the beginning. The whole day is before us.'

'The whole of life is before us. This *is* the beginning . . .'

'That is not what I meant. Tell me about the roots of your family, and the stem and the branches – and how you came to be Baal-Shazzur . . .'

'Very well. In the beginning, Zillah, El had a son who was King of Sidon. His name was Keret and he served the goddess Sapas. The land was rich and the people were happy. But there came a time when Sidon was threatened by not one army but by a league of armies. The Zebulonites and the Koserites marched against him and with them was Terah, the moon-god of Sidon; they laid waste all the ground they covered. Keret was a young man and though he was a trained warrior, skilled in all the arts of war, he had not a warrior's heart. He was a man who loved peace; he liked to walk in his fields and vineyards and lie on his back in the sun, listening to the crops growing; he liked to see his people fat and contented, to hear their voices singing as they reaped. When he heard that the armies of Terah were violating his borders, setting fire to the granaries and driving away all the cattle, his heart was so heavy that he could do nothing. He hid in his palace and wept. He was moved to sorrow but he was not yet moved to war. When he had wept until his eyes were blind he fell asleep and in his dream the goddess came to him and told him that he would one day father a son, as beautiful as Astarte, as gracious as Anat. He awakened to a world grown sweet with purpose and worth fighting for. Before he left the city at the head of his army he climbed to the summit of the sacred place and made his offering – wine in a silver cup, honey in a golden vase, the blood of a bird and the blood of a lamb.

'Belief in the future strengthens the arm. He vanquished the enemy and married a beautiful woman who gave him a son, as beautiful as Astarte, as gracious as Anat . . .'

'And *you* are descended from the son of King Keret of Sidon?'

'Zillah, my love, all slaves from the sea-coast of Canaan are descended from King Keret through the gift of the goddess. Who ever heard of a slave who had not royal blood in his veins?'

'Now you mock me.'

'Never, heart's breath. I may not be a prince descended from a god, but I was not always a slave. War deprived me of my freedom for a while but now I am rewarded for every miserable hour of slavery – my life, like King Keret's, is sweet with purpose. And had I lived out my years in my own house, in my own land, I would not now be a maker of most excellent pots, and the husband of Zillah, whom I have loved since she was a tiny girl with huge eyes.'

On the first morning of Zillah's absence Leah awakened to an unaccustomed silence. The sun has risen before my daughter, she thought – but Zillah's place was empty. Then I have slept too long, thought Leah, she has gone to the spring for water. But no. The great pitcher was where it always stood, and had been filled. The fire had been tended and fuel stacked nearby. But where was Zillah? Leah called on her neighbours and 'Yes,' they said, they had seen her. She was early abroad, it seemed, drawing water before the sun had appeared above the earth's rim. Perhaps the heat had prevented her from sleeping. Oh, a girl might have a thousand reasons for what she did, and no harm in any of them. She might be visiting friends, or helping with a cow in travail; the cows did not drop their calves as easily as in the old days.

'She would have told me,' Leah declared, but the women shook their heads and said, gently, 'Perhaps she did, Leah. Perhaps she did. You may have forgotten.'

Leah went back to her tent, anxious and doubtful. It was true she forgot many things; there was so little worth remembering when each day was empty. In Egypt, and even later, every chance event, however slight, was something to be stored and cherished, to relate with laughter to Ishvi as he ate. Now there was nothing, and why was that? She stood still and let the answer take possession of her mind though it opened doors she had closed many years before, though it let light into places she had kept comfortably shadowed. It was because Ishvi was not with her. Ishvi was dead! She threw herself upon the ground and wept. Her tears were like a river, all the tears she had held in check for so long and now let free. Her neighbours, hearing her sobbing, ran in to comfort her.

Young Adah, the daughter-in-law of Old Adah, the wife of Daniel, raised her in her arms and said, 'Hush, Leah. She will come back; there is no need to weep.' But another, more sensitive, said, 'She is weeping for Ishvi.'

It was a good and healing sorrow. When the tears abated and she could speak again, Leah said, 'I have been mad during all these years. I made a necessity of my grief as though it were food and drink – as though I had been born for no other purpose than to mourn my dead, and in such mourning keep alive my love. I have been closed in a tent of sorrow as securely as Prince Moses' god is confined in his sacred tabernacle. We have been carried along by the living and set down in this place and that place, and we are fed with sacrifice and *manna*. Because I would not loose my hold on Ishvi, I have lost my children. Where are Naboth and Naaman? Where is Zillah?'

'They are not lost,' said Adah. 'Naaman and Naboth are with Lord Joshua now. Naboth has married and his wife is near her time. You will have a grandson, Leah, so there is something to make you smile.'

'But my poor Zillah, who will marry her? I have kept her by me too long . . .'

Ah, that was hard to answer. 'Zillah is a good girl,' said Rachel, Adah's sister, 'a good daughter. Such virtue is a reward in itself.'

Leah sniffed, thinking the reward a poor substitute for married happiness. 'We shall see. Perhaps Naboth's wife has a brother? No? Well, we shall see.'

Here was something for her new mind to work on as she occupied her hands with the day's tasks, cooking, mending and spinning. Ishvi's shade had vanished from her fireside but she was not lonely at all, not even when night came and still Zillah had not returned.

The next day it was she who made excuses for her daughter's absence. The neighbours raised their eyebrows, thinking, 'But to stay away all night! Leah should take a rod to her shoulders . . .' The more charitable suggested that the girl had wandered away and been devoured by a lion, but Leah moved through the day untroubled by any such idea.

The lamp was lit and the stewed meat ready for eating when Zillah came home at last, leading Baal-Shazzur by the hand

and trembling a little at the thought of what her reception might be.

'Mother,' she said, her voice rather too loud and abrupt. 'This is my husband . . .' And Leah rose and kissed him, first one cheek and then the other.

'There is enough food for three,' she told them. 'The gods of the hearth guided my hand when I cut meat for the pot. But what nonsense is this about husbands? I have spent the hours since noon yesterday in planning what might be done for you, Zillah – and now it is all wasted.'

Then they were all laughing and talking at once until Leah said, 'I have not been so happy since before Ishvi's death,' and she put round Zillah's neck the collar of charms and amulets she had had from her own mother, Rebekkah, and wept again, but for joy.

20

The long journey continued. Younger shoulders bore the tabernacle's weight, younger arms strained at the ropes, tugging the pack-beasts on – and these new people sang as they marched.

Zillah bore a son and Naboth brought silver to press into his tiny fist. 'He will be a warrior,' said Naboth. 'See how he reaches out his hand for my spears.'

'He will be a potter,' said Zillah, firmly, and laughed at her brother's lordly dismay.

They swung up from the plains once more to the great oasis of Kadesh Barnea where Hamor and Dathan and Abirim had rebelled and died. That was only a memory among other memories, grown faint with time and distance.

Caleb, now a man in his prime, looked with longing at the green, rolling hills of the Negeb and thought he would willingly abandon his hope of Canaan to settle there, but he had vowed to serve Prince Moses and the Lord Joshua with his life, were that asked of him. Perhaps, later, he would return and make a separate peace with the hill-men.

Here Miriam died and was buried in a cave at the edge of the wasteland, and the precious relics of Ishtar's dance with her. After that there was no priestess among the Tribes, for Hannah had died of the plague and none of the younger women remembered the rite at all. A few old ones mourned and Zillah with them though she told no one why she did so. It was a secret between herself and Baal-Shazzur.

Canaan lay very near but, because of their earlier defeat, the people were reluctant to venture again into the Negeb. Moses fasted and kept his eyes from sleep until they sank deep in his head, but the god did not speak to him in any certain way. He did not say, 'Go against the hill-men!' and Moses would not take it upon himself to give that order. So they turned east again towards the Arabah and, on that stage of the journey, Aaron died.

His eldest son had been Yahweh's priest for many years, not taking Aaron's place but subject to him. Now the sacred garments of the high-priesthood were put about the younger man's shoulders, and Aaron's staff of office was put into his hand.

'May you serve Prince Moses' god better than I have served him,' said Aaron and Moses bent above his dying friend and said, 'You have served well for, of all the sons of Levi, only your staff has flowered. I have given the priesthood into your hands for ever.'

From Puron on the borders of Edom they passed to Oboth and from there to the southernmost extremity of the Salt Sea, a desolation of marsh and petrified vegetation, white salt-hills and withering heat. It was surely the land of the twin cities that the Great Spirit of Abram had destroyed. Might not any one of these strange, shining pillars contain the shadow of Lot's disobedient wife? The Israelites dreaded the thought of a march along its shore with no fodder for the beasts, no water that was drinkable. Moses had sweetened the waters of the desert with green boughs but no man could hope to sweeten so great a sea. Springs rose in the hills of Moab but their water evaporated long before they reached the level ground. It was death to stay here, death to go on, death to go back.

But these children of Israel were made of sterner stuff than their fathers, who would have died of despair in this appalling place, or turned against Prince Moses for the last time, cursing him, before going back to die against the spears of the hill-men.

These new Israelites grinned at each other through the thick, salt-laden mists, and whacked their beasts round and up, into the Kingdom of Sihon, into the hills east of the Salt Sea.

Furious, the King of Sihon sent out his armies against the impudent invaders – his best spearmen, his most victorious captains. And the Israelites tossed their own shining spears in the air and shouted, 'Yahweh!' and went on.

Leah sat with her grandchildren, Naboth's boys and Zillah's boy and the baby girl that was Baal-Shazzur's special delight, and she thought how strange it was that she should feel no fear. She wondered if it was one of the compensations of age, this unlooked-for calm when so great a battle was taking place nearby and her own sons in it. This time no one said to them, 'Fight!' but they fought. They were altogether a different race, she decided, her thoughts wandering. The generation that had died in the desert were of the old ways; they had not necessarily believed what the elders told them but they had obeyed. These free-born youngsters did not obey – but they believed. Ah, that was it. They were so armoured in belief they could not fail.

Absently she separated Naboth's sons who were having a battle of their own quite as desperate as the one that engaged their father. 'It is in you little ones that our hope lies,' she scolded. 'Be good now or your father shall hear of it!'

It was a great victory, a glorious victory. Because of it the Israelites walked taller in the world. They spread out from their first hurried camp until they had conquered the whole country around and then they went a little northward and defeated King Og of Bashan, a giant of a man with giants leading his armies.

At night they made songs around the fires and boasted of their prowess in battle and of the insatiable thirst of their spears; they added new verses to Miriam's old song of triumph, praising Yahweh for his aid against King Og and against the Ammorites. Even the children, who remembered Miriam only as an old, old woman with white hair and milky eyes, stamped and sang:

'Who is like Yahweh among all the gods?'

For Moses this was a time of mingled joy and sorrow. It was the end of the long journey, his dream's fulfilment, but it had taken too long and cost too much. He had thought to harness the god to his will and thereby rule the people who called themselves the Chosen of God – and it had been beyond his strength. The god had driven him hither and thither about the desert as the storm is driven; he had not revealed himself.

The air was filled with the noise of triumph, it beat about his head like wings and the reflected firelight, glancing from a thousand brandished spears, struck at his eyes like the lightning that had split the clouds on Mount Sinai the night of his marriage to Zipporah, Jethro's daughter.

Perhaps Zipporah was dead now as his little Cushite wife was dead – could he mourn one without the other? Yet his memory of Zipporah was faint while his heart still ached for the Cushite woman. Through her he had come to know, in his own flesh, the griefs of his people; he had held her in his arms and seen her fever-bright eyes glazed by death; he knew what Micael had felt, and Leah, and Aaron, and what a thousand others had felt as they scraped the dry soil over the corpses of husbands and wives, fathers, sons and daughters, leaving them in the graveyard of the desert.

And what now? Tomorrow they would descend from the hills and sit down in the plain of Jordan, across the river from Jericho. The real conquest was beginning, another lifetime would see it finished.

'Yahweh,' he whispered. 'What now? I have brought your people to the gate of the promised land . . .'

Almost before his words were truly formed the god answered him, the great voice pounding in his head, in his breast, in his belly, the words lost in the thunder of it. He felt the power shake him as though he had no more substance than a corn-doll. The voice was in himself but he could not hear it, he could not understand. He clutched his throat, trying to grasp with his hands the meaning of the sounds, and then he fell through circle after circle of black night until he found himself calm and still again, and the god had left him.

There was a bitterness in his mouth and his eyes did not see well but his mind was his own again. 'Joshua,' he said, and the name was heavy and awkward on his tongue. He tried again. 'Joshua.' It was easier, but slow, an eternity stretching between the picture in his head and the syllables ponderously shaped. 'Joshua!'

'I am here, Prince.'

I had not remembered him so tall, thought Moses, nor with such a light behind him ... ah, but that is the fire. It plays tricks with size ... I've noticed it before ...

'Help me up,' he said, and Joshua's strong hand was beneath his elbow, Joshua's lean strength supporting his aching body. 'The day is almost upon us,' he said, smiling at his own helplessness.

Joshua nodded. 'Tomorrow, or the day after, you will lead the people into Canaan.'

Moses shook his head and stars exploded behind his eyes. 'Not so. You must take the command from me, Joshua. Yahweh will redeem his promise – but it is not for me ...'

Joshua bent his head close to hear and Moses thought, He is just such a man as I was once, long ago in Egypt, before the link was forged between my life and Israel.

'Yahweh will speak to you,' he said. 'In you and in your seed will the covenant be honoured ...'

Then he slept. Joshua watched by him for a long time, brooding on the weight of responsibility that was now his – not the battles alone, he could win battles enough to put a whole empire in his hand – but there was more to conquest than fighting. Having conquered Canaan he must rule it. Without experience and without the wisdom a king inherited from the long line of his fathers, with no more than the strength of his spear-arm and his soldier's mind he must divide and govern a rich country with a seacoast stretching from Gaza to the city of Tyre and always be alert lest the dispossessed people find a leader amongst themselves and rise against him and the captains he would set above them. And he must also guide and rule the people of Israel.

Prince Moses slept and smiled. 'The god will speak to me,' Joshua said, aloud. 'But how can you know that so surely? Is the god's voice a part of the command you have relinquished?'

Suddenly he was restless to put it to the trial. Tomorrow or the next day they would move down to the plains and there they would rest a while and plan. He would risk nothing whether the god were with him or not; his warriors trusted him. I can take Jericho, he thought, the taking of a city proves nothing. I will send spies into the city and when the time is right I will take it – and who will know whether the god speaks through me as he spoke through Moses?

'Give me a sign, great Bull of Israel,' he said. 'Give me a sign that all the people can see. Show them, when we have taken Jericho, that I am true heir to Moses. Bid the sun stand still in the sky . . .'

He groaned and buried his head in his hands. That was no good beginning – to order the god who himself ordered all things. 'Prince Moses,' he whispered, reproachfully, 'could you have chosen no other man?'

21

The next day Moses called all the leaders of the people together and bade them follow Joshua, as they had followed him. He said this wryly for he had found them a proud and obstinate people, hard to lead and impossible to please. Yet he was sorry to let them go.

'I am too old to take you further,' he said.

Naboth said, 'Prince Moses, you will live for ever. My sons will carry spears in your service.'

And Moses answered, 'Let your sons serve Joshua, and let your grandsons serve Joshua's heirs. The future has no end.'

The whole camp was afire with the news. Some thought it a good thing, remembering the suffering they had known under Moses' leadership. 'With Joshua to lead us, our sons will live to be old men,' they said, 'though our fathers and our brothers died with the beards still downy on their cheeks. Joshua is one of us . . .'

But others remembered that Prince Moses had fed them in the desert, conjured water from solid rock and quails from the sky. 'Lord Joshua will take us across the silver river – but it was Prince Moses who brought us from Egypt.'

There were few now who remembered that day clearly. Most of them had been children and hardly aware of what was happening; with the older survivors memory was an uncertain thing, making much of some events and cancelling others as though they had never been. Leah thought most often of her father-in-law, Kedemah the Wealthy who, at the end, would have bartered all he had ever owned for one drop of water to wet the baby Naaman's lips – and Naaman did not remember him at all. His first memory was of his mother standing in the tent weeping, her hands at her sides and the tears falling unchecked and, apart from that, a general picture of heat and discomfort. Naboth had forgotten the heat and thirst; the image that stayed in his mind was of Prince Moses sweetening bitter water with branches torn from a low shrub. Zillah remembered two things that ran together – the first was of an evening when she sat on her father's knees while he told her about Lot and his wife and chided her for interrupting, the second was of a kind, wise man who had made her a dish with a grasshopper on it, long since lost. But now she had Baal-Shazzur who had made the dish, she had no need of memories.

They were all glad that the journey was over, that was one certain thing; they were glad to come down from Hebron and pitch their tents on the green plain beside the river, knowing that in a very little while they would take possession of all the land on the other side. The city could not long resist the victors of the high hills.

Already spies had crossed the expanse of shining water, had slipped within the city walls, were even now questioning the inhabitants, whispering, bribing. Joshua sat in his tent with his captains and the priests, planning the campaign. He was a great leader, a splendid leader, leaving nothing to chance and, moreover, he understood people, he knew their limitations and their strengths. Prince Moses had chosen wisely in the end; he had done his best all through, no doubt, but he had been harsh and sometimes cruel. 'After all, he is an Egyptian,' said Young Adah as though that explained everything, and Leah caught her breath, a faint memory stirring from far back. 'He is an Egyptian,' she agreed, and the memory tugged harder. But not hard enough.

Moses saw that they were happy with their new leader, ready to follow him until the next generation was grown, the

184

generation of the fulfilled covenant. Then there would be a time of judges and then a time of kings. But Israel was gathered home and safe.

He would not take his place on Joshua's council. 'I will go once more into the hills and praise Yahweh,' he said, and refused Joshua's offer of a man to go with him. Joshua shrugged and let him go, but anxiety for the old man stayed in his mind all day so that when evening came he himself went to bring him home.

It was early when Moses left the camp. The sun was risen but the whole world still had a freshness about it as though it were new-born. Dew drenched his feet and the spiders' webs that hung in the long grass were jewelled with glittering drops. The sun climbed with him, its heat increasing with every step he took. When he looked back he could see the camp far below, tiny people moving between the tents, animals like children's abandoned toys. The silence of distance lay between them and himself. And there was Jordan, shining silver, greater than any river except the Nile, flowing between the people and the land that was theirs.

'And it is not for me,' he said, aloud. 'It is not for me.' For many years he had struggled to make his spirit meek and it had been far from easy; now in his age he had learned to accept, but not with humility.

'Oh, Yahweh!' he cried. 'I am one with the generation that died in the wilderness. My bones will whiten with theirs, this side of the Jordan – but let my *ka* at least go free before the people into Canaan!'

Then he waited. The stillness was so profound he could hear his heart thudding behind his ribs, and there was no answer, not even from the secret place in his mind where the god had spoken before.

Rage possessed him. 'You put the command on me,' he shouted and shook his fists at the empty sky. '*You* made me the leader of this people, whether I would or no. You were *their* god, from the beginning of time, but they learned your will from *my* mouth. Well, God, Great Spirit, Rider of the Storm, here are your people, free-born, spear-hard . . . take them!' He opened his clenched hands and threw himself upon the ground and wept, tearing at the grass with his fingers, smelling the sweetness of the crushed blades.

'I have come a long way from the Nile that cradled me,' he groaned. 'I have suffered too, and hungered and thirsted. I have died with every death, mourned with every family, no loss was less to me than to them, though they were not my own people . . . not my own? They were my brothers and sisters . . .'

Again he waited while the silence flowed back; no sudden thunder came to shatter its calm. The god was not to be coaxed into speech.

This time Moses let the silence have its way. He was too weary to wrestle the god's voice out of the deep unknown as he had done before. He, who had once been Ra-Mose of Egypt, had finished with it all – the leadership, the sacred charge, the Law – let someone else now take it from his shoulders. Let Joshua seek the god with fire and sacrifice.

Bitterly he remembered how he had said, so long ago, 'I will harness this bull of Midian . . .' but which of them had harnessed which? Who was led and who driven? It was more than he cared to think about so near the end.

Steadying himself with the palms of his hands flat on the earth, he struggled to his knees and looked about him. He knelt in a green, sloping pasture scattered with flowers and half-enclosed by a rough natural wall of rock. Red anemones seemed to pant in the sun's heat and all the surrounding hills were swathed in colour. He stood upright and wondered at so much beauty, such an abundance of rich life.

'Lord God,' he breathed. 'I have lived to see the varied richness of your earth. Let me now see your face.'

A flurry of tiny birds rose from the grass in a frantic whirring of wings, their voices shrill with alarm, and Moses turned to see what had disturbed them. He turned slowly for he was an old man with aching bones and he had left his staff there on the ground where he had lain. He thought that perhaps an enemy had come upon him, a warrior from Jericho with a fierce, painted face and a spear poised to kill. Well, they would meet as men; a staff would not avail him. But it was not a man. There, in the opposite corner of the field, between two outcrops of rock, stood a bull, head low and massive shoulders humped. Moses could see the snort of breath from the wide, red-shadowed nostrils. The birds called to each other and spun down from the sky to resume their interrupted feast, searching for insects even between the hooves of the great beast.

Sudden tears coursed down the old man's cheeks.

'Lord Yahweh,' he said. 'I have searched for you so long . . .' and he went forward, his hands held out in greeting.

The bull took him on his horns and flung him skywards. For one brief instant that stretched, it seemed, into eternity, Moses hung spreadeagled on the air and saw, beyond Jordan and beyond Jericho, the whole rich land like a painted papyrus scroll beneath him – palms and vineyards and grain, from the white mountains to the shores of the Western Sea.

Then his body struck the ground and was still, his eyes still open on the wonders he had seen but a thin trickle of blood staining the corner of his mouth. The bull lowered his head and touched Moses' breast with his horns, almost tenderly, as though it were a caress.

Joshua found the body and buried it there where it had fallen, casting some of the earth behind him to appease Moses' spirit that would be held to the spot by the blood that had come from his mouth. It was a very little blood, not enough to anger the earth, but it was better to acknowledge it. When the work was finished Joshua saluted with his spear and went down again to the camp.

'Prince Moses walks with the god,' he said. But later he admitted that the Prince was dead, and the people mourned for the requisite number of days.

When the time of mourning was over they crossed the Jordan and set up their tents a little distance from the city walls.

22

It was the morning of the seventh day. At dawn Lord Joshua went out from the camp and seven priests went with him, each bearing a trumpet made from the horn of a ram. Behind them was carried the ark of the covenant of God concealed in its ragged tent of skins. As the sun rose higher in the sky, all the other people left their tents and shelters and followed the priests towards Jericho, to march round the outer walls of the city, to add their voices to the voices of the horns when Joshua should give the command.

Thus they had marched every day for six long days under the hot sun, the young and elderly together, women and warriors and children. Even the very little ones were there, some scarce able to walk alone, hand in hand with older brothers and sisters or clinging to their mothers, half-afraid.

Only old Leah stayed behind among the deserted tents. Jericho meant little to her; perhaps it was, as they said, the end of all the wandering, perhaps not – but she had spent too long in the wilderness to care very much either way. Most of those she had loved had left their bones back there, hidden beneath the cairns and mounds that marked the way from Egypt. Aye, most of her kin and all of her friends were dead. Even Prince Moses was dead, they told her.

She was old and her eyes were dry, the tear-ducts parched by years of white sunlight and shifting sand. In Egypt she had wept for her father, putting dust on her head and tearing her garments, and wept again for her mother, impatient Rebekkah. Later she had wept for her husband's brothers, one after the other, and then for her husband when she came to admit that he was dead. But for Prince Moses she could not weep.

She was too old. She looked down at her gnarled feet with their corded and knotted veins, the nails thick, ridged and curved like the talons of a bird, and she thought how those same feet had been young once and danced in honour of the sprouting barley. It was at the barley feast that Ishvi had first looked at her; it was on the last night, the night of the scattering, that they had joined hands across the golden sheaves. But that was in the old time, in Egypt, before Prince Moses had dreamed his dream.

'Eh, Ishvi, what a dream that was!' she said, and then remembered again that she was alone. But if only Ishvi were here, how they would laugh together to think that it was finished at last, all the trouble, the anxiety. With Ishvi's strong arm to support her, she too might have made the effort and circled the city, chanting. But without him nothing was any use.

'Well, Ishvi, my love,' she said, companionably, 'you were right and I was wrong. I never believed that we would get here – yet here I am. And our children and grandchildren all together. Naboth's boys are like tall saplings and they are loving and quarrelsome at the same time – they will make fine generals. Zillah has a husband who is a man after your own heart – true, he is a foreigner, but good as bread. She has a boy and a girl and another boy . . .' Leah counted them on her fingers. 'That is five grandchildren, Ishvi. Little Naaman married late. He also chose a foreigner, a girl from the hills above the Salt Sea, though Prince Moses forbade such marriages. I did not understand her at first for she speaks with a lisping tongue, but she is a gentle girl and will be a good mother when her time comes. No, Ishvi, I never believed it would happen. Even now Egypt is more real to me . . .'

Closing her eyes she could still see, quite clearly, that flat brown land, and still smell the brackish waters of the marsh where wild-fowl nested. She dozed and, between sleeping and waking, saw the rafts and reed-boats plying to and fro along the Nile, and she heard the voices of her parents raised in the old familiar argument:

'... they hid their sons from the Egyptians. They hid them in the granary and in caves and among the reeds at the river's edge. And some were found and killed ... and some were saved!'

Some were saved! She started awake and the fugitive memory that had eluded her since the day Prince Moses gave the command to Joshua slid into place. Some were saved!

A mother had wrapped her baby in fine linen and put him in a little ark made of reeds and smeared with pitch, floating him away on the slow water, into the night. Perhaps the crocodile, old Sebek, had taken him between his great jaws and that was the end. But perhaps Sebek had slept and the cradle had been drawn from the water by a woman of Pharaoh's household. Perhaps Prince Ra-Mose of Egypt had, after all, drawn his first breath in a tent of the Hebrew, been slapped into life by a Hebrew midwife – but who, now, would know? For Miriam was dead, and Aaron was dead, and there was no one at all who could say certainly who Prince Moses had been. Israelite or Egyptian, he had been a rare dreamer. Let him walk with his god.

From Jericho came the noise of a great shout, all the people shouting together with one voice, and the ram's horns blowing, and the thunder of stones falling.

And Leah slept again.